To the immortal Jane, with love and laughter
—PJ and DG

Contents

Volume III

Chapter One

IT IS A TRUTH universally acknowledged, that a handsome young tom in possession of his own territory must be in want of a mate.

"My dear Mr. Bennet!" said Mrs. Bennet. "Have you heard the news? Netherfield Park is marked at last! What a fine thing it would be for any of our five kittens to catch a rich mouse—I mean spouse," said Mrs. Bennet. "Really, Mr. Bennet, you must pay a call on Mr. Bingley immediately, before that scheming Lady Lucas pounces on him for her daughter Charlotte."

What a fine thing it would be for any of our five kittens to catch a rich mouse—I mean spouse.

Mr. Bennet, however, feigned indifference, yawning and proceeding to wash his face.

"I'll tell you what, my dear," said he, "why don't you go yourself? I will send a few lines by you to assure Mr. Bingley of my hearty consent to his marrying whichever he chooses of our daughters; though I must throw in a good word for my little Lizzy."

"I desire you will do no such thing. Lizzy is not a bit better than the others; I am sure she has neither Jane's fluffiness nor Lydia's animal spirits. But you are always giving *her* the preference."

Mr. Bennet steadfastly refused to call on Mr. Bingley, and his wife's mournful meows could be heard echoing through the halls of Longbourn. She was as nervous as a cat has a right to be about finding her kittens good mates. For, if she did not succeed in marrying her daughters off to rich toms, she would be thrown out to the hedgerows to catch her own supper when Mr. Bennet died.

Poor Mrs. Bennet was a cat of dim perceptions and horrifying hallucinations. The business of her life was to see her kitties well-mated; its solace was visiting and mews.

It is a truth universally acknowledged, that a single man in possession of a good fortune, must be in want of a wife.

However little known the feelings or views of such a man may be on his first entering a neighbourhood, this truth is so well fixed in the minds of the surrounding families, that he is considered the rightful property of some one or other of their daughters.

Chapter Two

OBSERVING HIS SECOND daughter attacking a feathered bonnet, Mr. Bennet remarked, "I hope Mr. Bingley will like it, Lizzy."

"We are not in a way to know what Mr. Bingley likes," sniffed Mrs. Bennet, "since we are not to visit."

"But you forget, Mama," said Elizabeth, "that we shall frolic with him at the assemblies."

At that moment, Kitty began coughing up a hairball.

Kitty began coughing up a hairball.

"Not another hairball, Kitty, for heaven's sake!" cried Mrs. Bennet. "Have a little compassion on my poor nerves!"

"Kitty has no discretion in her hairballs," said her father. "She times them ill."

"When is your next hair ball—I mean ball to be, Lizzy?"

"Tomorrow fortnight."

Mr. Bennet suggested they return to the subject of Mr. Bingley.

But now poor Mrs. Bennet found *herself* coughing up a hairball. "I am sick of Mr. Bingley!" she gagged.

"I am sorry to hear that; but why did not you tell me before?" replied her husband. "If I had known as much this morning, I certainly would not have called on him. It is very unlucky; but as I have actually paid the visit, we cannot escape the acquaintance now."

Upon hearing this, Mrs. Bennet frisked and frolicked with abandon; the irksome hairballs were entirely forgotten. Instead, her head was filled with visions of the coming assembly. There, in the ball room, her daughters would meet the alluring Mr. Bingley and, if all went as planned, enjoy the pleasure of chasing the ball (Sir William Lucas had procured a particularly fine one with a bell inside) under the sideboard with him. These hopes and expectations raised Mrs. Bennet's spirits to a pleasant pitch, for such sport with such a partner promised to answer all her dearest hopes for the happines of at least one of her daughters, and the security of the entire family.

"What an excellent father you have, girls," said she, when the door was shut. "I do not know how you will ever make him amends for his kindness; or me either for that matter. At our time of life it

is not so pleasant, I can tell you, to be making new acquaintances every day; but for your sakes, we would do any thing. Lydia, my love, though you are *the youngest, I dare say Mr. Bingley will dance with you at the next ball."*

Chapter Three

THOUGH HE HAD visited Mr. Bingley, Mr. Bennet did not give his family the satisfaction of a description of their new neighbor. Was he long or short-haired, remote or cuddly? Did he sleep on or under the bed? The five Bennet sisters could only speculate on these fascinating questions. But their curiosity would soon be satisfied, for Mr. Bingley would be attending the assembly ball.

"If I can but see one of my kittens happily purring at Netherfield," said Mrs. Bennet to her husband, "and all the others equally well-mated, I shall have nothing to yowl about."

Mrs. Bennet invited Mr. Bingley to dine at Longbourn and planned a marvelous meal of mouse tails and spiced mole. But Mr. Bingley, drooling for a big-city rat, ambled off to London without warning. Mrs. Bennet was quite put out. Was he forever to be straying here and there instead of curling up contentedly at Netherfield?

When the evening of the ball came, Mr. Bingley arrived with his two sisters: Mrs. Hurst and Miss Caroline Bingley. Also accompanying him was his friend, Mr. Darcy, a handsome cat with an equally handsome fortune of 10,000 mice a year and an extra six lives into the bargain.

"What a catch for our girls!" chirped Mrs. Bennet.

As it turned out, Mr. Darcy was a proud, disdainful cat who looked down on country kitties and growled when Mr. Bingley suggested he ask Elizabeth to prance! Fortunately, Mr. Bingley was more accommodating, for he delighted in the company of country cats and romped spiritedly around the room with Jane. After supper, all the cats, with the exception of the proud Mr. Darcy, played with a handsome ball with a bell inside, and an excellent ball it was!

"*Come, Darcy,*" *said he, "I must have you dance. I hate to see you standing about by yourself in this stupid manner. You had much better dance.*"

"*I certainly shall not. You know how I detest it, unless I am particularly acquainted with my partner. At such an assembly as this, it would be insupportable. Your sisters are engaged, and there is not another woman in the room, whom it would not be a punishment to me to stand up with.*"

"*I would not be so fastidious as you are,*" *cried Mr. Bingley, "for a kingdom! Upon my honour, I never met with so many pleasant girls in my life as I have this evening; and there are several of them you see uncommonly pretty.*"

"*You* are dancing with the only handsome girl in the room," *said Mr. Darcy, looking at* [Jane], *the eldest Miss Bennet.*

"*Oh! She is the most beautiful creature I ever beheld! But there is one of her sisters sitting down just behind you, who is very pretty, and I dare say very agreeable. Do let me ask my partner to introduce you.*"

"*Which do you mean?*" *and turning round he looked for a moment at Elizabeth, till catching her eye, he withdrew his own and coldly said: "She is tolerable, but not handsome enough to tempt* me; *and I am in no humour at present to give consequence to*

She is tolerable, but not handsome enough to tempt *me*.

young ladies who are slighted by other men. You had better return to your partner and enjoy her smiles, for you are wasting your time with me."

JANE WAS WARM in her praise of Mr. Bingley after meeting him at the assembly.

"He is just what a tom cat ought to be," said she, "and he has his breeding papers, too."

"He also has street smarts," said Elizabeth, "since he spends a good part of his time in the sewers—that is, since he spends a good part of the *season* in town."

"His sisters are pleasing, too," said Jane. "Miss Bingley is to keep Netherfield free of mice. What a charming neighbor!"

Miss Bingley is to keep Netherfield free of mice.

9

Elizabeth said nothing. Privately, she thought the two Bingley sisters proud and conceited. They were of a respectable breeder in the north, a circumstance more deeply impressed on their memories than that their brother's fortune of 5,000 mice a year had been acquired not by hunting, but by trade!

Between [Bingley] *and Darcy there was a very steady friendship, in spite of great opposition of character—Bingley was endeared to Darcy by the easiness, openness, and ductility of his temper, though no disposition could offer a greater contrast to his own, and though with his own he never appeared dissatisfied. On the strength of Darcy's regard Bingley had the firmest reliance, and of his judgment the highest opinion. In understanding, Darcy was the superior. Bingley was by no means deficient, but Darcy was clever. He was at the same time haughty, reserved, and fastidious, and his manners, though well-bred, were not inviting. In that respect his friend had greatly the advantage. Bingley was sure of being liked wherever he appeared, Darcy was continually giving offense.*

WITHIN A SHORT walk of Longbourn lived a family with whom the Bennets were particularly intimate. Sir William Lucas had risen to the honor of cathood and the distinction gave him many airs.

Charlotte Lucas was a close friend of Elizabeth's, and that the two families would meet to talk over the ball (especially one with a bell inside) was absolutely necessary.

Everyone agreed that Mr. Bingley admired Jane Bennet exceedingly. He had pranced with her twice!

"Still," said Mrs. Bennet, feigning indifference as she licked her paw, "it may all come to nothing you know."

Mr. Bingley pranced with Jane twice!

They discussed Mr. Darcy who, everyone agreed, was eaten up by a pride—that is, eat up with pride (for, luckily, no lions had attacked him).

"If I had 10,000 mice a year like Mr. Darcy," said one of Charlotte's younger brothers, "I should drink a bottle of cream every day and keep a pack of hounds."

"Hounds, how horrible!" cried Mrs. Bennet with a shudder. "They would chase you all over the countryside."

"I should outrun them," declared the young tom. Mrs. Bennet continued to exclaim over the horror of hounds, and the dispute ended only with the visit.

"[Darcy's] *pride,*" *said Miss Lucas, "does not offend me so much as pride often does, because there is an excuse for it. One cannot wonder that so very fine a young man, with family, fortune, everything in his favour, should think highly of himself. If I may so express it, he has a* right *to be proud."*

"*That is very true,*" replied Elizabeth, "*and I could easily forgive his* pride, *if he had not mortified* mine."

"*Pride,*" observed Mary, who piqued herself upon the solidity of her reflections, "*is a very common failing I believe. By all that I have ever read, I am convinced that it is very common indeed, that human nature is particularly prone to it, and that there are very few of us who do not cherish a feeling of self-complacency on the score of some quality or other, real or imaginary. Vanity and pride are different things, though the words are often used synonymously. A person may be proud without being vain. Pride relates more to our opinion of ourselves, vanity to what we would have others think of us.*"

THE KITTIES OF Longbourn soon waited on those of Nether-field. The visit was returned in due form. Miss Bennet's pleasing mannerisms grew on the goodwill of Mrs. Hurst and Miss Bingley, though Mrs. Bennet was found to be intolerable, and the younger sisters not worth sniffing. Elizabeth still saw superciliousness in the Bingley sisters' treatment of everybody, hardly excepting even Jane, and could not like them.

It was generally evident that Mr. Bingley did admire Jane and equally evident that Jane was in a way to be very much in love; but Elizabeth considered with pleasure that Jane was not a demonstrative cat, and her preference was not likely to be discovered by the world in general. She mentioned this to her friend Charlotte Lucas, who only shook her head.

"If a cat conceals her affection with the same skill from the object of it, she may lose the opportunity of securing a home. Who will want to pet and pamper such a cat?" she said. "Jane should therefore make the most of every half hour in which they are playing or napping to command his attention."

"But Jane has known Bingley only a fortnight," said Elizabeth. "She romped with him at Meryton and shared a bowl of wet food with him in company four evenings. Those four evenings have enabled them to ascertain that they both like Purina better than

Fancy Feast, but with respect to any other leading characteristic, I do not imagine that much has been unfolded."

A few days later, the neighboring cats gathered at Lucas Lodge. Occupied in observing Mr. Bingley's attentions to her sister, Elizabeth was far from suspecting that she was herself becoming an object of some interest in the eyes of his pedigreed friend. No sooner had Mr. Darcy made it clear to himself that she hardly had a good feature in her face, than he began to find it was rendered uncommonly intelligent by the beautiful expression of her luminous eyes. And, in spite of his asserting that her manners were not those of an aristocat, he was caught by their easy playfulness as she chased a ball of yarn under the table.

Elizabeth then proceeded to pounce on the piano and the other cats pranced around the drawing room. Mr. Darcy watched in silence.

"What a charming amusement this is for young cats, Mr. Darcy!" said Sir William Lucas. "I consider prancing as one of the first refinements of polished society."

"Certainly, sir; and it has the advantage also of being in vogue amongst the less polished societies of the world. Every alley cat can prance."

"You have a house in town, I conclude?" asked Sir William.

Mr. Darcy yawned.

"I once had some thought of getting fixed in town (by an eminent veterinarian of our acquaintance) so Lady Lucas would not be disturbed by my nightly prowls."

Soon afterwards, Miss Bingley approached Mr. Darcy.

"Imagine," said she, "the insipidity, and yet the yowls—the nothingness, and yet the self-importance—of all these country cats! What would I give to hear your strictures on them!" growled Caroline.

Mr. Darcy assured her that his mind was more agreeably engaged in admiring Elizabeth Bennet's beautiful eyes.

"Miss Elizabeth Bennet!" repeated Miss Bingley. "I am all astonishment. I've heard she's a good mouser, too, so that settles the matter. Pray, when am I to wish you joy?"

"A female's imagination is very rapid," remarked Mr. Darcy drily. "It jumps from admiration to mice, and from mice to matrimony, in a moment."

Convinced by his manner that all was safe where Elizabeth was concerned, Miss Bingley spent the rest of the evening trilling to Mr. Darcy and preening herself by the fire.

**The insipidity, and yet the yowls—the nothingness,
and yet the self-importance—of all these country cats!**

"*Happiness in marriage is entirely a matter of chance* [said Charlotte to Elizabeth]. *If the dispositions of the parties are ever so well known to each other, or ever so similar before-hand, it does not advance their felicity in the least. They always contrive to grow sufficiently unlike afterwards to have their share of vexation; and it is better to know as little as possible of the defects of the person with whom you are to pass your life.*"

"*You make me laugh, Charlotte; but it is not sound. You know it is not sound, and that you would never act in this way yourself.*"

Longbourn, Mr. Bennet's territory, produced 2,000 juicy mice a year. The entire estate was end-tailed to a male hair, unfortunately for the Bennet sisters, for Mr. and Mrs. Bennet had produced only female litters.

The two youngest kitties, Catherine and Lydia, had craniums even smaller and more vacant than those of other cats. They rollicked and romped here and there without a rational idea in their heads. Indeed, these empty-headed kits were filled with rapture upon learning that an army of toms were to camp in the neighborhood for the entire winter! What flouncing and pouncing they anticipated, what bells and balls! Mr. Bingley's large fortune paled beside the vision of a red-coated, red-blooded tom.

Kitty and Lydia romped here and there without a rational idea in their heads.

Their father just shook his head.

"From all I can collect by your manner of romping," he observed, "you must be two of the silliest cats in the country."

Later that day, a footcat came in with a note for Miss Jane Bennet. It was an invitation from the two Bingley sisters to dine at Netherfield, though the tomcat of the house would be out.

At that moment, something quite remarkable occurred. A thought popped into Mrs. Bennet's tiny brain—that Jane go on horseback to Netherfield so that if by lucky chance it rained, she would have to stay overnight.

This plan was quickly implemented, with the result that Jane ended up thoroughly drenched, with her beautiful fur all flattened. The Bingley sisters remarked snidely that she looked like a drowned rat. She was obliged to remain at Netherfield, and the doctor forced a nasty pill down her throat—without even a juicy pill pocket to make it go down easily!

The next morning, Elizabeth trotted through the wet fields to visit her sister, getting her white paws very muddy in the process.

Poor Jane was so ill that Elizabeth was invited to stay at Netherfield to nurse her. A servant was promptly sent out on a chase across four fields (known as a chase and four) to fetch Elizabeth's belongings and return to Netherfield.

[Elizabeth] *was shewn into the breakfast-parlour, where all but Jane were assembled, and where her appearance created a great deal of surprise—That she should have walked three miles so early in the day, in such dirty weather, and by herself, was almost incredible to Mrs. Hurst and Miss Bingley; and Elizabeth was convinced that they held her in contempt for it. She was received, however, very politely by them; and in their brother's manners there was something better than politeness; there was good humour and kindness—Mr. Darcy said very little, and Mr. Hurst nothing at all. The former was divided between admiration of the brilliancy which exercise had given to her complexion, and doubt as to the occasion's justifying her coming so far alone. The latter was thinking only of his breakfast.*

Chapter Eight

AT HALF-PAST SIX, Elizabeth was summoned to dinner: an array of freshly opened cans of succulent tuna and chicken livers in gravy.

The Bingley sisters were tolerably agreeable at dinner. But Mr. Hurst was a lazy cat who lived only to eat, drink, and conk out; who, when he found Elizabeth to prefer dry food to a fresh-killed rodent, had nothing to say to her.

When dinner was over, Miss Bingley began abusing Elizabeth as soon as she was out of the room. Her purr was not pleasing; she had no style, no taste, no papers. Mrs. Hurst thought the same, and added, "She has nothing, in short, to recommend her, but being an excellent stalker. Did you see her with that bird in her mouth? She really looked almost wild."

"To walk three miles, or four miles, or five miles, or whatever it is, above her paws in mud. What could she mean by it? It seems to me to show a most country-cat indifference to decorum."

When Elizabeth came down in the evening, she found Miss Bingley purring vigorously on the subject of Mr. Darcy's sister, Georgiana.

"How I long to see Georgiana again! Such a countenance, such manners! And so extremely accomplished for a kitten! She pounces exquisitely on the pianoforte."

"It is amazing to me," observed Bingley, "how young female cats can have the patience to be so very accomplished as they all are."

She really looked almost wild.

"All cats accomplished! My dear Charles, what do you mean?"

"Yes, all of them, I think. They all walk across fresh paint, making delightful paw marks, stretch out full-length on a table, obstructing their owners' plans, and claw net purses to pieces."

"Oh! Certainly," cried Caroline, "a cat must have a thorough knowledge of purring, yowling, and leaping . . . and besides all this, she must possess a certain something in her hair and manner of stalking."

"And to all this," added Mr. Darcy, "she must yet add extensive napping."

"I am no longer surprised at your knowing only *six* accomplished cats," said Elizabeth. "I rather wonder now at your knowing any!"

Her manners were pronounced to be very bad indeed, a mixture of pride and impertinence; she had no conversation, no style, no taste, no beauty. Mrs. Hurst thought the same, and added,

She must possess a certain something in her hair and manner of stalking.

"She has nothing, in short, to recommend her, but being an excellent walker. I shall never forget her appearance this morning. She really looked almost wild."

"She did, indeed, Louisa. I could hardly keep my countenance. Very nonsensical to come at all! Why must she be scampering about the country, because her sister had a cold? Her hair, so untidy, so blowsy!"

"Yes, and her petticoat; I hope you saw her petticoat, six inches deep in mud, I am absolutely certain; and the gown which had been let down to hide it, not doing its office."

"Your picture may be very exact, Louisa," said Bingley; "but this was all lost upon me. I thought Miss Elizabeth Bennet looked remarkably well, when she came into the room this morning. Her dirty petticoat quite escaped my notice."

"You observed it, Mr. Darcy, I am sure," said Miss Bingley; "and I am inclined to think that you would not wish to see your sister make such an exhibition."

"*Certainly not.*"

"*To walk three miles, or four miles, or five miles, or whatever it is, above her ankles in dirt, and alone, quite alone! what could she mean by it? It seems to me to shew an abominable sort of conceited independence, a most country town indifference to decorum.*"

"*It shows an affection for her sister that is very pleasing,*" said Bingley.

"*I am afraid, Mr. Darcy,*" observed Miss Bingley in a half whisper, "*that this adventure has rather affected your admiration of her fine eyes.*"

"*Not at all,*" he replied; "*they were brightened by the exercise.*"

To all this, she must yet add extensive napping.

Chapter Nine

POOR JANE CONTINUED to feel very low. She hid in the back of the closet and was not even up to batting around a crumpled piece of paper that Elizabeth discovered under the fender. Consequently, Mrs. Bennet and her two youngest kittens descended upon Netherfield to visit Jane. It was decided that Jane would stay on until her condition improved and the apothecary ordered some succulent chicken pill pockets, for Jane preferred these to the nasty salmon-flavored ones that Miss Bingley had procured from the cook.

"I do not know a place that is equal to Netherfield," remarked Mrs. Bennet, as she entered the breakfast parlor. "You will not think of quitting it in a hurry, I hope, Mr. Bingley, though you do have but a short leash."

Meanwhile, Lizzy spotted a mouse and pounced on it.

"Lizzy!" cried her mother. "Remember where you are, and do not run in the wild manner that you are suffered to do at home!"

The cats then compared the merits of country life to living in town.

"The city," observed Mr. Darcy, "has fat, tasty rats as well as mice."

"I assure you," retorted Mrs. Bennet, "there is quite as much of *that* going on in the country as in town."

Mr. Darcy merely gazed at her and commenced licking his paw, and Mrs. Bennet fancied she had scored a triumph.

Lizzy spotted a mouse and pounced on it.

They then discussed the efficacy of cheese versus grain in trapping mice.

"I have been used to consider cheese the very food of entrapment," said Mr. Darcy.

"A fine, stout Stilton may be," said Elizabeth. "But a mild low-fat cheddar may chase a mouse entirely away."

Before they left, Lydia, in high animal spirits, reminded Mr. Bingley of his promise to give a dance with plenty of balls. He replied that he would, just as soon as Jane's fur fluffed up again, and Lydia could name the day.

"The country," said Darcy, "can in general supply but a few subjects for such a study. In a country neighbourhood you move in a very confined and unvarying society."

"But people themselves alter so much, that there is something new to be observed in them for ever."

"*Yes, indeed,*" cried Mrs. Bennet, offended by his manner of mentioning a country neighbourhood. "*I assure you there is quite as much of that going on in the country as in town.*"

Every body was surprised; and Darcy, after looking at her for a moment, turned silently away. Mrs. Bennet, who fancied she had gained a complete victory over him, continued her triumph.

. . .

"*Aye—that is because you have the right disposition. But that gentleman,*" looking at Darcy, "*seemed to think the country was nothing at all.*"

"*Indeed, Mama, you are mistaken,*" said Elizabeth, blushing for her mother. "*You quite mistook Mr. Darcy. He only meant that there was not such a variety of people to be met with in the country as in the town, which you must acknowledge to be true.*"

"*Certainly, my dear, nobody said there were; but as to not meeting with many people in this neighbourhood, I believe there are few neighbourhoods larger. I know we dine with four and twenty families.*"

Chapter Ten

WHEN ELIZABETH CAME downstairs after dinner, she began to chew on some embroidery, being careful not to get a needle stuck in the roof of her mouth, as had happened to a cat of her acquaintance.

While this was going on, Miss Bingley swatted Mr. Darcy with her paw, harassing him as he tried to compose a letter to his sister. Mr. Bingley observed that Mr. Darcy did not write with ease; he studied too much for words of four syllables. (Darcy *was* fond of a dictionary, but he sprawled on it even more often than he looked *into* it.) Mr. Bingley on the other hand always walked carelessly across his letters while the ink was still wet, blotting them horribly.

"Everything I do is done quickly," trilled Mr. Bingley, attacking a dormouse scurrying across the floor.

Darcy and Bingley proceeded to spar over the merits of pouncing quickly versus reflecting first. Bingley observed that Darcy always got the upper paw in these disputes.

"I assure you, that if Darcy were not such a magnificently tall tom, in comparison with myself, I should not pay him half so much deference. I declare," said Mr. Bingley, "I do not know a more awful object than Darcy, on particular occasions, and in particular places; at his own house especially, and of a Sunday evening, when he has nothing to bat about."

I do not know a more awful object than Darcy at his own house especially, and of a Sunday evening, when he has nothing to bat about.

Miss Bingley and her sister then caterwauled a duet and Elizabeth could not help noticing how often Mr. Darcy's eyes were fixed on her. When Miss Bingley varied the charm by a lively Scottish-fold air, Darcy drew near her.

"Are you not tempted by the lively music, Miss Bennet, to join me in unraveling a fishing reel?"

Elizabeth declined, and Mr. Darcy really believed that were it not for the inferiority of her cat connections in London, he should be in some danger.

"I hope," said [Miss Bingley], *as* [she and Mr. Darcy] *were walking together in the shrubbery the next day, "you will give your mother-in-law a few hints, when this desirable event takes place, as to the advantage of holding her tongue; and if you can compass it, do cure*

the younger girls of running after officers—And, if I may mention so delicate a subject, endeavour to check that little something, bordering on conceit and impertinence, which your lady possesses."

"Have you anything else to propose for my domestic felicity?"

"Oh! yes—Do let the portraits of your uncle and aunt Philips be placed in the gallery at Pemberley. Put them next to your great uncle the judge. They are in the same profession, you know; only in different lines. As for your Elizabeth's picture, you must not have it taken, for what painter could do justice to those beautiful eyes?"

"It would not be easy, indeed, to catch their expression, but their colour and shape, and the eyelashes, so remarkably fine, might be copied."

Do let the portraits of your uncle and aunt Philips be placed in the gallery at Pemberley. Put them next to your great uncle the judge.

Chapter Eleven

JANE WAS NOW well enough to go down to the pawing room with Elizabeth and the Bingley sisters. Mr. Bingley cavorted with joy at seeing Jane all fluffed up again!

No one wanted to chase string or bat cards about, so Mr. Hurst stretched out on one of the sofas and took a catnap. Mr. Darcy was engaged in a book, and Miss Bingley took the second volume of his and sprawled across it with a great yawn.

"How pleasant it is to spend an evening in this way! I declare, after all there is no enjoyment like stretching oneself over a book so our humans have no chance of reading it! How much sooner one tires of anything else but this! When I have a house of my own, I shall be miserable if I have not an excellent library.

"By the bye, Charles, are you really serious in meditating a great ball at Netherfield? Although these lowly country cats would be most amused with a ball, I would advise you, before you determine on it, to consult the wishes of the present party; I am much mistaken if there are not some among us to whom a ball would be rather a punishment than a pleasure."

"If you mean Darcy," cried her brother, "he may go to bed, if he chooses, before it begins—but as for the ball, it is quite a settled thing; and as soon as Nicholls has made rat-atouille enough, I shall send round my cards."

"A ball would be infinitely more rational," replied Miss Bingley, "if it was not round or did not roll."

"Much more rational, my dear Caroline, I dare say, but it would not be near so much like a ball."

Miss Bingley made no answer; and soon afterwards got up and walked about the room. Her figure was elegant, and she walked well—but Darcy, at whom it was all aimed, was still inflexibly studious.

Her figure was elegant and she walked well.

In the desperation of her feelings she resolved on one effort more; and, turning to Elizabeth, said,

"Miss Eliza Bennet, let me persuade you to follow my example, and take a turn about the room. I assure you it is very refreshing after sitting so long in one attitude."

Elizabeth was surprised, but agreed to it immediately. Miss Bingley succeeded no less in the real object of her civility; Mr. Darcy looked up. He was as much awake to the novelty of attention in that quarter as Elizabeth herself could be, and unconsciously closed his book. He was directly invited to join their party, but he declined it, observing, that he could imagine but two motives for their choosing to walk up and down the room together, with either of which motives his joining them would interfere. "What could he mean? she was dying to know what could be his meaning"—and asked Elizabeth whether she could at all understand him?

"Not at all," was her answer; "but depend upon it, he means to be severe on us, and our surest way of disappointing him, will be to ask nothing about it."

Chapter Twelve

THE NEXT MORNING, Elizabeth and Jane determined to leave Netherfield, lest they overstay their welcome.

This communication elicited fresh invitations to prolong their stay. Mr. Bingley chirped encouragingly, while Miss Bingley chimed in with a half-hearted meow. Till the morrow, then, their going was deferred. Miss Bingley was sorry that she had acceded to the delay, for her jealousy and dislike of one sister much exceeded her affection for the other.

Mr. Bennet, though very laconic in his expressions of pleasure, was really glad to see Jane and Elizabeth when they arrived home the next day; he had felt their importance in the family circle. The evening cavorting, while they were away at Netherfield, had lost much of its animation and almost all its cat sense with their absence.

[Mr. Bingley] *heard with real sorrow that they were to go so soon, and repeatedly tried to persuade Miss Bennet that it would not be safe for her—that she was not enough recovered; but Jane was firm where she felt herself to be right.*

To Mr. Darcy it was welcome intelligence—Elizabeth had been at Netherfield long enough. She attracted him more than he liked—and Miss Bingley was uncivil to her, *and more teazing than usual to himself. He wisely resolved to be particularly careful that no sign of admiration should now escape him, nothing that could elevate her with the hope of influencing his felicity; sensible that if such an idea had been suggested, his behaviour during the last day must have material weight in confirming or crushing it.*

Chapter Thirteen

THE NEXT MORNING Mr. Bennet informed his wife that he was expecting a gentleman and a stranger at dinner.

"Good lord!" exclaimed Mrs. Bennet. "How unlucky! There is not a bit of carp to be got today. Lydia, my love, perhaps you and Kitty can catch some in the goldfish pond."

Mr. Bennet went on to explain that the mysterious visitor was his cousin, Mr. Collins, who, as soon as Mr. Bennet was dead, could turn the Bennet family out into the hedgerows to scramble for mice on their own.

"Pray do not talk of that odious cat," hissed Mrs. Bennet. "I do think it is the hardest thing in the world that your estate should be end-tailed away from your own kittens."

It is the hardest thing in the world that your estate should be end-tailed away from your own kittens.

Jane and Elizabeth tried to explain to their mother the immutable nature of an end-tail. They had often attempted to do it before, but it was a subject on which Mrs. Bennet was beyond the reach of reason.

"It certainly is a most iniquitous affair," said Mr. Bennet, "and nothing can clear Mr. Collins from the guilt of inheriting Longbourn. But if you will listen to his letter and his offer of an olive branch, you may perhaps be a little softened by his manner of purring."

"I think it is very impertinent of him to communicate with you at all," said Mrs. Bennet. "Why could he not keep on having cat fights with you, as his father did before him?"

Mr. Bennet then proceeded to read Mr. Collins's letter:

"Dear Sir,

"The constant territorial disputes subsisting between yourself and my late honored father always gave me much uneasiness, and since I have had the misfortune to lose him, I have frequently wished to heal the breach. Therefore, if you should have no objection to receive me into your house, I propose myself the satisfaction of waiting on you and your family."

Mr. Collins went on to say that he should arrive at Longbourn that very day.

"In point of composition," observed Mary, "the letter does not seem defective. Though I must say, I prefer a ball of yarn to an olive branch."

Mr. Collins arrived punctually, duly bearing the olive branch, which Lydia and Kitty immediately leapt at.

Cousin Collins lost no time in complimenting Mrs. Bennet on the beauty of her five kittens.

"Yes, but the poor things will have to fend for themselves when their father dies," observed Mrs. Bennet. "Mr. Bennet's estate is settled so oddly."

"You allude, perhaps, to the end-tail of this estate," said Mr. Collins, swishing his tail.

"Ah! Sir, I do indeed. There is no knowing how estates will go when once they come to be end-tailed."

Mr. Collins assured Mrs. Bennet that he came prepared to admire her five daughters and perhaps transport one back to his humble abode in Hunsford, replete with mouse holes fitted up very nicely by his noble patroness, Lady Cat.

Mrs. Bennet's dinner, too, in its turn, was excessively admired; and he begged to know to which of his fair cousins the excellency of its cooking was owing. But he was set right there by Mrs. Bennet, who assured him with some asperity that they were very well able to keep a good cook, and that her daughters had nothing to do in the kitchen, although, she confessed, Lydia had snagged the goldfish in the pond that morning.

~~~❊~~~

"Dear Sir,

"The disagreement subsisting between yourself and my late honoured father, always gave me much uneasiness, and since I have had the misfortune to lose him, I have frequently wished to heal the breach; but for some time I was kept back by my own doubts, fearing lest it might seem disrespectful to his memory for me to be on good terms with any one with whom it had always pleased him to be at variance. . . My mind, however, is now made up on the subject, for having received ordination at Easter, I have been so fortunate as to be distinguished by the patronage of the Right Honourable Lady Catherine de Bourgh, widow of Sir Lewis de Bourgh, whose bounty and beneficence has preferred me to the valuable rectory of this parish, where it shall be my earnest endeavour to demean myself with grateful respect towards her ladyship, and be ever ready to perform those rites and ceremonies which are instituted by the Church of England. As a clergyman, moreover, I feel it my duty to promote and establish the blessing of peace in all families within the reach of my influence; and on these grounds I flatter myself that my present overtures of good will are highly commendable, and that the circumstance of my being next in the entail of Longbourn estate, will be kindly overlooked on your side, and not lead you to reject the offered olive-branch. I cannot be otherwise than concerned at being the means of injuring your amiable daughters, and beg leave to apologise for it, as well as to assure you of my readiness to make them every possible amends—but of this hereafter. If you should have no *objection to receive me into your house, I propose myself the satisfaction of waiting on you and your family, Monday, November 18th, by four o'clock, and shall probably trespass on your hospitality till the Saturday se'night following, which I can do without any inconvenience, as Lady Catherine is far from objecting to my occasional absence on a Sunday, provided that some other clergyman is engaged to do the duty of the day. I remain, dear sir, with respectful compliments to your lady and daughters, your well-wisher and friend,*

"WILLIAM COLLINS"

Chapter Fourteen

"YOU APPEAR TO be very fortunate in your patroness, Lady Cat," remarked Mr. Bennet to his cousin after dinner.

Mr. Collins protested that "he had never in his life witnessed such behaviour in a cat of rank—such affability and cat-descension." Lady Cat's attention to everything from his choice of cushions to his brand of kitty litter all appeared very remarkable. Indeed, her consideration was beyond anything he could have anticipated. She had asked him twice to hunt shrews at Rosings, and had sent for him only the Saturday before to make up her pool of quadrille in the evening. She had even condescended to advise him to mate as soon as he could, provided he chose with discretion; and had once paid him a visit in his humble parsonage, where she had perfectly approved all the alterations he had been making, and had even vouchsafed to suggest a superior style of scratching post for his drawing room.

"It is a pity that great cats in general are not more like her," observed Mrs. Bennet. "Does she live near you, sir?"

"The garden in which stands my humble abode is separated only by a lane from Rosings Park!" trilled Mr. Collins.

"I think you said she was a widow, sir? Has she any family?"

"She has only one kitten, the hairess of Rosings"

"Ah!" said Mrs. Bennet, shaking her head, "then she is better off than many cats. And what sort of puss is she?"

The garden in which stands my humble abode is separated only by a lane from Rosings Park!

"She is a most charming cat indeed. Lady Cat herself says that, in point of true beauty, Miss de Bourgh is far superior to the handsomest of her pedigree, because there is that in her furry face which marks the cat of a distinguished breed. She is unfortunately of a sickly constitution, which has necessitated frequent trips to the vet. However, the cost is of no account to Lady Cat. And though more than one person has suggested putting Miss de Bourgh down, her ladyship will not hear of it."

"Has she been presented? I do not remember her name among the ladies at court."

"Her indifferent state of health unhappily prevents her being in town; and by that means, as I told Lady Catherine myself one day, has deprived the British court of its brightest ornament. Her ladyship seemed pleased with the idea, and you may imagine that I am happy

on every occasion to offer those little delicate compliments which are always acceptable to ladies. I have more than once observed to Lady Catherine, that her charming daughter seemed born to be a duchess, and that the most elevated rank, instead of giving her consequence, would be adorned by her—These are the kind of little things which please her ladyship, and it is a sort of attention which I conceive myself peculiarly bound to pay."

"You judge very properly," said Mr. Bennet, "and it is happy for you that you possess the talent of flattering with delicacy. May I ask whether these pleasing attentions proceed from the impulse of the moment, or are the result of previous study?"

"They arise chiefly from what is passing at the time, and though I sometimes amuse myself with suggesting and arranging such little elegant compliments as may be adapted to ordinary occasions, I always wish to give them as unstudied an air as possible."

Chapter Fifteen

Mr. Collins was not a sensible cat, and the deficiency of nature had been but little assisted by training, the greatest part of his life having been spent under the guidance of an irascible, ill-bred father. The subjection in which his father had brought him up had originally given him great humility of manner; but it was now a good deal counteracted by the self-conceit of a tiny brain over-powered by feelings of self-importance.

He planned on choosing a mistress for Hunsford, whom Lady Cat would approve of—a modest, useful cat who could amble daily across the lane to Rosings with him. He was hoping to select one of the Bennet sisters as a plan of atonement for inheriting their father's estate. At first he fixed on the fluffy Jane, but Mrs. Bennet gave him a hint that she might soon be spoken for. Mr. Collins had only to change from Jane to Elizabeth—and it was soon done while Mrs. Bennet was grooming herself in front of the fire.

The next day Mr. Collins accompanied the Bennet sisters on a walk to Meryton—much to Mr. Bennet's relief, since Mr. Collins had followed him to his library after breakfast and stretched out on one of his largest folios with a yawn, looking as if he intended to stay the entire morning.

In Meryton, the attention of the female cats was caught by a young tom of most elegant appearance whom the Bennet sisters had never seen before, walking with a red-coated cat of their

Mr. Collins stretched out on one of Mr. Bennet's folios with a yawn.

acquaintance. All were struck with the stranger's hair, which was sleek and shiny, and wondered who he could be; and Mr. Denny introduced the handsome-whiskered tom as Mr. Wickham. The whole party were mewing together very agreeably, when Darcy and Bingley were seen trotting down the street. Mr. Darcy was beginning to determine not to fix his eyes on the frisky Elizabeth, when he was suddenly arrested by the sight of the stranger, and Elizabeth, happening to see both as they looked at each other, was all astonishment at the effect of the meeting. The hair on each stood up, and Mr. Darcy growled. What could be the meaning of it?

Mrs. Philips [Mrs. Bennet's sister] *was always glad to see her nieces; and the two eldest, from their recent absence, were particularly welcome, and she was eagerly expressing her surprise at their*

sudden return home . . . when her civility was claimed towards Mr. Collins by Jane's introduction of him. She received him with her very best politeness, which he returned with as much more, apologising for his intrusion, without any previous acquaintance with her, which he could not help flattering himself however might be justified by his relationship to the young ladies who introduced him to her notice. Mrs. Philips was quite awed by such an excess of good breeding; but her contemplation of one stranger was soon put to an end by exclamations and inquiries about the other; of whom, however, she could only tell her nieces what they already knew, that Mr. Denny had brought him from London, and that he was to have a lieutenant's commission in the _____ shire. She had been watching him the last hour, she said, as he walked up and down the street, and had Mr. Wickham appeared Kitty and Lydia would certainly have continued the occupation, but unluckily no one passed the windows now except a few of the officers, who in comparison with the stranger, were become "stupid, disagreeable fellows." Some of them were to dine with the Philipses the next day, and their aunt promised to make her husband call on Mr. Wickham, and give him an invitation also, if the family from Longbourn would come in the evening. This was agreed to, and Mrs. Philips protested that they would have a nice comfortable noisy game of lottery tickets, and a little bit of hot supper afterwards.

Chapter Sixteen

UPON ENTERING MRS. Philips's rooms with his cousins, Mr. Collins was immediately struck with the size and elegance of the furniture. Why, he could walk under the sideboard without flattening himself in the least! The elegance of the apartments brought to mind Lady Cat's pawing room where the chimney piece alone cost 800 mice!

The Bennet sisters were relieved when Mr. Wickham strolled into the room, for he was far beyond the other toms in catness, countenance, hair, and stride. Even his "mews" were rendered interesting by his skill in delivering them.

Wickham and Elizabeth were soon engaged in an intriguing conversation concerning Mr. Darcy. Wickham confirmed that Darcy was a most proud and disagreeable tom in spite of his fine figure and lush coat. In fact, said Wickham, he had been most ill-used by Mr. Darcy.

"I have been a disappointed cat, and my spirits will not bear solitude," he confessed.

When the elder Mr. Darcy died, Wickham confided, he had bequeathed Wickham a field of catnip, 1,000 cans of Fancy Feast, and two extra lives, since old Mr. Darcy had only used seven of his own. However, the son (the present Mr. Darcy) had contrived to cheat Wickham out of this rich inheritance despite the fact that Wickham and Darcy were born in the same dresser drawer and

I have been a disappointed cat, and my spirits will not bear solitude.

spent the greatest part of their kittenhood wrestling and kicking each other!

"This is quite shocking! Mr. Darcy deserves to be publicly disgraced," cried Elizabeth.

On the carriage ride home, Elizabeth could think of nothing but what Wickham had related, while Lydia, her head full of the evening's entertainment, talked incessantly of the fish she had lost and the fish she had won.

Allowing for the common demands of the game, Mr. Wickham was therefore at leisure to talk to Elizabeth, and she was very willing to hear him, though what she chiefly wished to hear she could not

hope to be told, the history of his acquaintance with Mr. Darcy. She dared not even mention that gentleman. Her curiosity however was unexpectedly relieved. Mr. Wickham began the subject himself. He inquired how far Netherfield was from Meryton; and, after receiving her answer, asked in an hesitating manner how long Mr. Darcy had been staying there.

"About a month," said Elizabeth; and then, unwilling to let the subject drop, added, "He is a man of very large property in Derbyshire, I understand."

"Yes," replied Mr. Wickham—"his estate there is a noble one. A clear ten thousand per annum. You could not have met with a person more capable of giving you certain information on that head than myself—for I have been connected with his family in a particular manner from my infancy."

Elizabeth could not but look surprised.

"You may well be surprised, Miss Bennet, at such an assertion, after seeing, as you probably might, the very cold manner of our meeting yesterday—Are you much acquainted with Mr. Darcy?"

"As much as I ever wish to be," cried Elizabeth very warmly,—"I have spent four days in the same house with him, and I think him very disagreeable."

. . .

"I cannot pretend to be sorry," said Wickham, after a short interruption, "that he or that any man should not be estimated beyond their deserts; but with him *I believe it does not often happen. The world is blinded by his fortune and consequence, or frightened by his high and imposing manners, and sees him only as he chooses to be seen."*

"I should take him, even on my *slight acquaintance, to be an ill-tempered man." Wickham only shook his head.*

"I wonder," said he, at the next opportunity of speaking, "whether he is likely to be in this country much longer."

"I do not at all know; but I heard nothing of his going away when I was at Netherfield. I hope your plans in favour of the _____shire will not be affected by his being in the neighbourhood."

"Oh! no—it is not for me to be driven away by Mr. Darcy. If he wishes to avoid seeing me, he must go. We are not on friendly terms, and it always gives me pain to meet him, but I have no reason for avoiding him but what I might proclaim to all the world, a sense of very great ill usage, and most painful regrets at his being what he is. His father, Miss Bennet, the late Mr. Darcy, was one of the best men that ever breathed, and the truest friend I ever had; and I can never be in company with this Mr. Darcy without being grieved to the soul by a thousand tender recollections. His behaviour to myself has been scandalous; but I verily believe I could forgive him anything and every thing, rather than his disappointing the hopes and disgracing the memory of his father."

Chapter Seventeen

TENDER-HEARTED JANE WAS shocked to hear the unfortunate tale of Darcy and Wickham from Elizabeth the next morning, and couldn't help but to feel that it was all due to a terrible misunderstanding, as sometimes subsists between two toms.

In the meantime, all the Bennet sisters were cheered by the thought of the splendid ball Mr. Bingley was planning to procure. It was said to be rather large and to contain a hint of catnip and two silver bells. Even Mary made no objection to the innocent, if vacuous, amusement such a ball must bestow.

"While I can nap all morning," said she, "it is no sacrifice to join occasionally in an evening frolic."

Elizabeth's spirits were so high that she actually asked Mr. Collins if he intended to accept Mr. Bingley's invitation, and if he did, whether he would think it proper to play with the ball; she was rather surprised to find that he entertained no scruple whatever on that head, and was very far from dreading a rebuke either from the Archbishop or Lady Cat.

"I am by no means of the opinion, I assure you," said he, "that a ball of this kind, procured by a cat of character, can have any evil tendency; and I am so far from objecting to rolling the ball about myself, that I shall hope to be honoured with the paws of all my fair cousins in the course of the evening; and I take this opportu-

nity of soliciting yours, Miss Elizabeth, for the two first bounces especially."

Elizabeth felt herself completely taken in.

She had fully proposed being engaged by Mr. Wickham for those very bounces; and to have Mr. Collins instead—her liveliness had never been worse timed! Moreover, she began to suspect that she had the dubious honor of being selected as worthy of being the mistress of Hunsford Parsonage and of assisting to form a quadrille table at Rosings in the absence of more eligible cats.

The prospect of the Netherfield ball was extremely agreeable to every female of the family. Mrs. Bennet chose to consider it as given

in compliment to her eldest daughter, and was particularly flattered by receiving the invitation from Mr. Bingley himself, instead of a ceremonious card. Jane pictured to herself a happy evening in the society of her two friends, and the attention of their brother; and Elizabeth thought with pleasure of dancing a great deal with Mr. Wickham, and of seeing a confirmation of everything in Mr. Darcy's looks and behavior. The happiness anticipated by Catherine and Lydia, depended less on any single event, or any particular person, for though they each, like Elizabeth, meant to dance half the evening with Mr. Wickham, he was by no means the only partner who could satisfy them, and a ball was, at any rate, a ball. And even Mary could assure her family that she had no disinclination for it.

Chapter Eighteen

ELIZABETH WAS MOST disappointed with Mr. Bingley's much-talked of ball because Wickham was not there to roll or run with it. Not only that, but she had promised Mr. Collins the first two bounces!

Elizabeth was astonished when Mr. Darcy asked her for a bounce, and endeavored to converse with him as little as possible until it occurred to her that she could torment him more effectively by obliging him to speak. She then made some slight observation on the splendor of the ball.

"It is your turn to talk now, Mr. Darcy," she said.

"Do you talk by rule then, while at play?" he asked.

"We are each of an unsocial, taciturn disposition," replied Elizabeth, "and are unwilling to open our mouths unless it is to utter such a meow as will amaze the whole room."

"This is no striking resemblance of your own catness," he said.

"We have tried two or three subjects already without success," observed Elizabeth, "and what we are to talk of next I cannot imagine."

"What think you of newts?" said he, smiling.

"Newts—oh! No. I am sure we never stalk the same, or not with the same feelings."

"I am sorry you think so; but if that be the case, there can at least be no want of subject. We may compare our different opinions."

"No—I cannot talk of newts in a ball-room; my head is always full of something else."

Elizabeth then spoke of Darcy's mistreatment of Wickham. Just as she anticipated, Darcy's tail swished and his eyes flashed. But he did not attempt to defend himself.

After the dance, Caroline Bingley approached Elizabeth. "Wickham's encroaching on Mr. Darcy's territory was a most insolent thing, but considering he is descended from a common alley cat, one could not expect much better," she said.

"His guilt and his descent appear by your account to be the same," retorted Elizabeth.

"Excuse my interference," spat Miss Bingley, "it was kindly meant."

At supper, Mrs. Bennet yowled triumphantly of her expectation of Jane's marrying Mr. Bingley, while Darcy looked grave. Mary plunked on the pianoforte with very little grace, and Lydia and Kitty exposed themselves with the officers. To make matters worse, Mr. Collins hardly left Elizabeth's side, sorely tempting her to swat him with her paw.

[As Elizabeth and Darcy danced] *Sir William Lucas appeared close to them, meaning to pass through the set to the other side of the room; but on perceiving Mr. Darcy he stopt with a bow of superior courtesy to compliment him on his dancing and his partner.*

"I have been most highly gratified indeed, my dear Sir. Such very superior dancing is not often seen. It is evident that you belong to

Such superior dancing is not often seen.

the first circles. Allow me to say, however, that your fair partner does not disgrace you, and that I must hope to have this pleasure often repeated, especially when a certain desirable event, my dear Eliza, (glancing at her sister and Bingley,) shall take place. What congratulations will then flow in! I appeal to Mr. Darcy—but let me not interrupt you, Sir. You will not thank me for detaining you from the bewitching converse of that young lady, whose bright eyes are also upbraiding me."

The latter part of this address was scarcely heard by Darcy; but Sir William's allusion to his friend seemed to strike him forcibly, and his eyes were directed with a very serious expression towards Bingley and Jane, who were dancing together.

THE NEXT DAY opened a new scene at Longbourn. Mr. Collins solicited a private audience with Lizzy who, however, endeavored to scamper away.

"Lizzy, I insist upon your staying and hearing Mr. Collins!" ordered Mrs. Bennet.

As soon as they were alone, Mr. Collins said to Lizzy: "Believe me, my dear Miss Elizabeth, that your modesty, so far from doing you any disservice, rather adds to your other purrfections."

The next moment, Mr. Collins's animal instincts got the best of him, for he ran away after a mouse that had scurried under a chair. He soon recollected himself, however.

"Almost as soon as I entered the house, I singled you out as the companion of my future life," he assured Lizzy solemnly. "Twice," continued he, "has Lady Cat condescended to meow pointedly (unprovoked too!) on this subject; and it was but the very Saturday night before I left Hunsford—while we batted about a spool of thread—that she said, 'Mr. Collins, you must marry. Choose properly, choose a pure-bred for my sake; and for your own, let her be an active, useful sort of cat, able to make a small rodent go a good way. This is my advice. Find such a creature as soon as you can, bring her to Hunsford, and I will visit her.'"

"You will find her breeding beyond anything I can describe," Mr. Collins continued, "and your frisks and capers, I think, must

Don't come back
without a wife, either!

be acceptable to her, especially when tempered with the silence and subjection which her rank will inevitably excite."

Lizzy hastened to decline the honor of his paw, but Mr. Collins chose to see her refusal as a lady-like game of cat and mouse.

"I am perfectly serious in my refusal," cried she, batting a ball under the couch. "On my honor, I am not toying with you!"

Mr. Collins persisted in believing that Elizabeth meant to increase his love by suspense, according to the practice of elegant felines.

Exasperated, Lizzy decided she must apply to her father, whose behavior at least could not be mistaken for affectation and coquetry.

"My reasons for marrying are, first, that I think it a right thing for every clergyman in easy circumstances (like myself) to set the example of matrimony in his parish. Secondly, that I am convinced it will add very greatly to my happiness; and thirdly—which perhaps I ought to have mentioned earlier, that it is the particular advice and recommendation of the very noble lady whom I have the honour of calling patroness. Twice has she condescended to give me her opinion (unasked too!) on this subject; and it was but the very Saturday night before I left Hunsford—between our pools at quadrille, while Mrs. Jenkinson was arranging Miss de Bourgh's foot-stool, that she said, 'Mr. Collins, you must marry. A clergyman like you must marry. Choose properly, choose a gentlewoman for my sake; and for your own, let her be an active, useful sort of person, not brought up high, but able to make a small income go a good way. This is my advice. Find such a woman as soon as you can, bring her to Hunsford, and I will visit her.' Allow me, by the way, to observe, my fair cousin, that I do not reckon the notice and kindness of Lady Catherine de Bourgh as among the least of the advantages in my power to offer. You will find her manners beyond any thing I can describe; and your wit and vivacity I think must be acceptable to her, especially when tempered with the silence and respect which her rank will inevitably excite. Thus much for my general intention in favour of matrimony; it remains to be told why my views were directed towards Long-bourn instead of my own neighbourhood, where I assure you there are many amiable young women. But the fact is, that being, as I am, to inherit this estate after the death of your honoured father, (who, however, may live many years longer,) I could not satisfy myself without resolving to choose a wife from among his daughters, that the loss to them might be as little as possible, when the melancholy *event takes place—which, however, as I have already said, may not be for several years. This has been my motive, my fair cousin, and I flatter myself it will not sink me in your esteem. And now nothing remains for me but to assure you in the most animated language of the violence of my affection."*

Wait, Cousin Elizabeth! I have not yet assured you of the violence of my affection!

Chapter Twenty

MRS. BENNET POUNCED on Mr. Collins as soon as he was alone in the room. She was alarmed, however, upon hearing of Lizzy's refusal.

"Lizzy is a foolish cat and does not know dry food from wet," she cried. Then she hastened to Mr. Bennet's library and jumped up on his chair, which she often used as a scratching post. She began to sharpen her claws energetically.

Help, we are all in an uproar!

"Mr. Bennet, we are all in an uproar!" she screeched. "Lizzy has scampered away from Mr. Collins and now Mr. Collins threatens to run away from Lizzy!"

Mr. Bennet called the defiant Lizzy to his library.

"And so," he said, "you refuse to become the future companion of Mr. Collins; you decline the honor of making up a foursome at quadrille with her Ladyship?"

Elizabeth affirmed that she did.

To her relief, her father took her side. He then calmly requested that his wife remove her claws from his chair and allow him to curl up quietly by himself. This distressed Mrs. Bennet greatly. All her future plans for comfort and security had been cruelly overthrown, and her howls of protest and ill-usage echoed forlornly through the halls of Longbourn.

"I tell you what, Miss Lizzy—if you take it into your head to go on refusing every offer of marriage in this way, you will never get a

husband at all—and I am sure I do not know who is to maintain you when your father is dead—I shall not be able to keep you—and so I warn you—I have done with you from this very day—I told you in the library, you know, that I should never speak to you again, and you will find me as good as my word. I have no pleasure in talking to undutiful children—Not that I have much pleasure, indeed, in talking to anybody. People who suffer as I do from nervous complaints can have no great inclination for talking. Nobody can tell what I suffer— But it is always so. Those who do not complain are never pitied."

Chapter Twenty-One

WHILE MRS. BENNET persisted in scolding Elizabeth for refusing Mr. Collins's paw in marriage, Mr. Collins comforted himself by rolling around with Miss Lucas in some catnip grown expressly for him by Lady Cat's head gardener.

Meanwhile, Lizzy met Mr. Wickham and had a cozy chat with him about the ball at Netherfield. Both lamented that they had not had a chance to bounce it together around the ball room. What a romp they would have enjoyed!

Soon afterwards, Jane received a letter from Caroline Bingley. Miss Bingley wrote that her brother had left for London, and since

Jane received a letter from Caroline Bingley.

his friends did not want him to spend his vacant hours meowing despondently in some lonely kennel, they had all hastened to join him. What fine big rats they would catch in the sewers, now that the season had begun in town!

Although Caroline wrote in a lady-like hand, Elizabeth detected claw marks on the elegant, hot pressed paper. Catty Caroline teased Jane mercilessly about Georgiana Darcy's manifold attractions, and her expectation of Miss Darcy's marriage to Mr. Bingley. (Miss Darcy was said to be a well-grown young cat who was accomplished in chirruping, napping, and washing herself. What reasonable hope could Jane entertain of the pliable Mr. Bingley resisting such attractions?)

Elizabeth was confident that Mr. Bingley would be back in Hertfordshire very soon, but Mrs. Bennet was quite discomposed by the news that he had left Netherfield. She took comfort, however, in planning a supper for him of roasted harvest mouse that would, no doubt, lead him ere long to propose to Jane.

"When my brother left us yesterday, he imagined that the business which took him to London might be concluded in three or four days, but as we are certain it cannot be so, and at the same time convinced that when Charles gets to town, he will be in no hurry to leave it again, we have determined on following him thither, that he may not be obliged to spend his vacant hours in a comfortless hotel. Many of my acquaintance are already there for the winter; I wish I could hear that you, my dearest friend, had any intention of making one in the crowd, but of that I despair. I sincerely hope your Christmas in Hertfordshire may abound in the gaieties which that season generally brings, and that your beaux will be so numerous as to prevent your feeling the loss of the three of whom we shall deprive you. . . .

"Mr. Darcy is impatient to see his sister, and to confess the truth, we *are scarcely less eager to meet her again. I really do not think Georgiana Darcy has her equal for beauty, elegance, and accomplishments; and the affection she inspires in Louisa and myself, is heightened into something still more interesting, from the hope we dare entertain of her being hereafter our sister."*

Chapter Twenty-Two

Miss Lucas kept Mr. Collins distracted all day by engaging him in unraveling a ball of yarn. Elizabeth was grateful to be free of his sullen looks and injured air but little could she have surmised that Charlotte was possessed of a fierce ambition. She was, in short, determined to secure Mr. Collins for herself!

Indeed, sly Mr. Collins crept out of Longbourn at an early hour the next morning, and trotted down the lane towards Lucas Lodge. Miss Lucas herself perceived him from an upper window and

Mr. Collins crept out of Longbourn at an early hour.

scooted out to meet him "accidentally" in the lane. She little could have imagined what passionate caterwauls awaited her there!

Poor Mr. Collins, poor Miss Lucas! But though Mr. Collins was a dim-witted cat, he was also a respectable one. Miss Lucas could look forward to tidy kitty litter boxes in her new establishment, and eventually a litter of her own.

Charlotte charged Mr. Collins with uttering not one murmur about their agreement when he returned to Longbourn, and Mr. Collins promised, though it was hard for him not to publish his prosperous love to all the cats in the county.

When Charlotte did tell her the news, Elizabeth was shocked. How could her dear friend, an indubitably sensible cat, ever be happy with the empty purrs and false posturings of Cousin Collins?

Miss Lucas perceived him from an upper window.

"Engaged to Mr. Collins! My dear Charlotte—impossible!"

The steady countenance which Miss Lucas had commanded in telling her story, gave way to a momentary confusion here on receiving so direct a reproach; though, as it was no more than she expected, she soon regained her composure, and calmly replied,

"Why should you be surprised, my dear Eliza? Do you think it incredible that Mr. Collins should be able to procure any woman's good opinion, because he was not so happy as to succeed with you?"

But Elizabeth had now recollected herself, and making a strong effort for it, was able to assure her with tolerable firmness that the prospect of their relationship was highly grateful to her, and that she wished her all imaginable happiness.

"I see what you are feeling," replied Charlotte—"you must be surprised, very much surprised—so lately as Mr. Collins was wishing to marry you. But when you have had time to think it over, I hope you will be satisfied with what I have done. I am not romantic, you know. I never was. I ask only a comfortable home; and considering Mr. Collins's character, connections, and situation in life, I am convinced that my chance of happiness with him is as fair, as most people can boast on entering the marriage state."

Chapter Twenty-Three

Sir William Lucas lost no time in informing the Bennets of his daughter's good fortune in entrapping (as Mrs. Bennet regarded it) Mr. Collins for her future mate.

The news threw Mrs. Bennet into a pitiable state. She reduced Mr. Bennet's favorite chair to shreds at the thought of Mr. Collins and Charlotte mewing secretly in anticipation of the prosperous hour when they would assume possession of Longbourn. To

Lady Lucas came to triumph over Mrs. Bennet in quite a territorial manner.

further affront her, Mr. Collins sniffed all the Bennets' furniture and actually sprayed the rug in Mrs. Bennet's best parlour! Lady Lucas, too, came to visit often to triumph over poor Mrs. Bennet in quite a territorial manner.

"I cannot bear to think that Mr. Collins and Charlotte should have all this estate," Mrs. Bennet hissed to her husband. "Mr. Collins has a scrawny thin end-tail. It is nothing at all to Jane's, but because she is a female she is disregarded and Mr. Collins will go on marking my rugs and calculating the number of mice who inhabit our park. It is all quite insupportable!"

Mrs. Bennet was really in a most pitiable state. The very mention of any thing concerning the match threw her into an agony of ill humour, and wherever she went she was sure of hearing it talked of. The sight of Miss Lucas was odious to her. As her successor in that house, she regarded her with jealous abhorrence. Whenever Charlotte came to see them she concluded her to be anticipating the hour of possession; and whenever she spoke in a low voice to Mr. Collins, was convinced that they were talking of the Longbourn estate, and resolving to turn herself and her daughters out of the house, as soon as Mr. Bennet were dead. She complained bitterly of all this to her husband.

"Indeed, Mr. Bennet," said she, "it is very hard to think that Charlotte Lucas should ever be mistress of this house, that I should be forced to make way for her, and live to see her take her place in it!"

"My dear, do not give way to such gloomy thoughts. Let us hope for better things. Let us flatter ourselves that I may be the survivor."

"The work is rather too light & bright & sparkling;—it wants shade;—it wants to be stretched out here & there with a long Chapter—of sense if it can be had, if not of solemn specious nonsense—about something unconnected with the story; an Essay on Writing, a critique on Walter Scott, or the history of Buonaparte."

Jane Austen's letter to her sister Cassandra, 4 February 1813, commenting on *Pride and Prejudice*

Chapter One

JANE RECEIVED A second letter from Caroline Bingley in which her claw marks were even more pronounced than on the first, though Jane chose to overlook them. According to Miss Bingley, her brother and Georgiana Darcy were on the brink of a felicitous union of their respective nine lives (making a total of eighteen, unless, as a dashing young cat at Oxford, Mr. Bingley may happen to have forfeited one or two). The friends and well-wishers of the happy couple awaited the moment when their understanding would be announced—an event that must bring Caroline ever closer to becoming mistress of Pemberley.

As a dashing young cat at Oxford, Mr. Bingley may have forfeited one or two of his nine lives.

Elizabeth could feel nothing but indignation towards a cat, such as Mr. Bingley, who might sleep here or sleep there to oblige his designing friends and remain insensible to the fact that back at Longbourn, poor Jane was taking twenty-three-and-a-half-hour naps to avoid dwelling on what must only make her unhappy. Could, Elizabeth wondered, the irresolute Mr. Bingley really have forgotten his ball and the precious moments he spent rolling it under the dining room table with Jane?

Mrs. Bennet, meanwhile, complained constantly about how ill-used she was by all the cats in the kingdom. None of them had any regard for her poor nerves, or cared if her wet food was left out to get dry, or her favorite toy got lost under the sofa. To make matters worse, Lady Lucas, who was all out for what she could get, came on purpose to Longbourn one morning to show off an especially juicy vole she had captured, lording it over poor Mrs. Bennet who had hardly had the strength to lift a paw under the heavy weight of recent disappointments and reversals.

Mr. Wickham frequently kept company with the Bennets during this gloomy interval. Now that Mr. Darcy had left the neighborhood, Wickham became even less reserved in communicating all he had suffered at the paws of Mr. Darcy. By now, all the cats in the neighborhood were sensible of the injuries Wickham had endured, and all detested the proud ill-tempered Darcy, except for the mild-mannered Jane, who suggested he might merely (as is the case of many a seemingly ill-natured cat) be misunderstood.

Mrs. Bennet still continued to wonder and repine at his returning no more, and though a day seldom passed in which Elizabeth did not account for it clearly, there seemed little chance of her ever consid-

ering it with less perplexity. Her daughter endeavoured to convince her of what she did not believe herself, that his attentions to Jane had been merely the effect of a common and transient liking, which ceased when he saw her no more; but though the probability of the statement was admitted at the time, she had the same story to repeat every day. Mrs. Bennet's best comfort was that Mr. Bingley must be down again in the summer.

Mr. Bennet treated the matter differently. "So, Lizzy," said he one day, "your sister is crossed in love I find. I congratulate her. Next to being married, a girl likes to be crossed in love a little now and then. It is something to think of, and gives her a sort of distinction among her companions. When is your turn to come? You will hardly bear to be long outdone by Jane. Now is your time. Here are officers enough in Meryton to disappoint all the young ladies in the country. Let Wickham be your man. He is a pleasant fellow, and would jilt you creditably."

"Thank you, Sir, but a less agreeable man would satisfy me. We must not all expect Jane's good fortune."

"True," said Mr. Bennet, "but it is a comfort to think that whatever of that kind may befal you, you have an affectionate mother who will always make the most of it."

Chapter Two

WHILE ALL THIS was going on at Longbourn, Mr. Collins was preparing to receive his bride at Hunsford, and he couldn't help peering through the opening in the trees that allowed him a glimpse of Rosings in ecstatic anticipation of sharing the view with his dear Charlotte.

At Christmas, Mrs. Bennet's brother, a sensible and well-mannered cat whose cranium was considerably larger than his sister's, came to visit with his wife, Mrs. Gardiner, a particular favorite with Jane and Elizabeth. Caroline Bingley and her sister would not have believed that Mr. Gardiner, who lived within view of a *warehouse* (where he had great sport in catching rats), could be so amiable and respectable.

The sight of the visitors elicited fresh wails of ill-usage from Mrs. Bennet who, all during their visit, never relaxed her protestations on the general perverseness of life. Two daughters on the brink of marriage—and it had all come to nothing!

During their stay, Lizzy discussed with Aunt Gardiner Jane's recent disappointment over Bingley.

"It had better have happened to *you*, Lizzy; you would have frisked and frolicked yourself out of it sooner. But do you think she would be prevailed upon to go back to town with us? A change of scene and relief from your mother's plaintive meows might be of service."

You, Elizabeth, would have frisked and frolicked yourself out of it sooner.

Jane readily agreed to the plan.

The Gardiners stayed a week at Longbourn and what with the noise and confusion of neighboring cats coming and going, they never got the comfort of a quiet bowl of crunchies by themselves.

Mrs. Bennet had so carefully provided for the entertainment of her brother and sister, that they did not once sit down to a family dinner. When the engagement was for home, some of the officers always made part of it, of which officers Mr. Wickham was sure to be one; and on these occasions, Mrs. Gardiner, rendered suspi-

cious by Elizabeth's warm commendation of him, narrowly observed them both. Without supposing them, from what she saw, to be very seriously in love, their preference of each other was plain enough to make her a little uneasy; and she resolved to speak to Elizabeth on the subject before she left Hertfordshire, and represent to her the imprudence of encouraging such an attachment.

Chapter Three

MRS. GARDINER TOOK the opportunity of a private conference with Elizabeth to warn her to be on her guard with the handsome Mr. Wickham, whose relative poverty (thanks a lot, Mr. Darcy!) rendered him an unsuitable match for her niece.

Elizabeth bantered with her aunt, reminding her that the want of a comfortable, secure home never prevented two kitties from entering into the marriage state, especially when the moon was full.

Mr. Collins and Charlotte's wedding day approached. Charlotte paid a farewell visit to Longbourn during which Mrs. Bennet favored her with sour looks and ill-natured growls. Elizabeth felt ashamed of her mother's bad breeding and spectacular stupidity in refusing to understand the intractable nature of an entail. Charlotte, however, appeared not to notice; she was simply pleased with Elizabeth's promise to visit Hunsford in March.

Meanwhile, in London, Jane waited in vain for a visit from Caroline Bingley. Every morning began with Jane putting out a fresh sardine in anticipation of seeing her friend, and every evening ended with her making a fresh excuse for Caroline's continued absence. Finally, both sardines and excuses grew stale, and after a brief, chilly visit from Miss Bingley, Jane sadly confessed to Elizabeth that she had been deceived in Caroline's character—catty she was, and catty she had long been and, Jane feared, duplicitous too.

Back at Longbourn, Wickham withdrew his attentions from Elizabeth to bestow them on a young feline who had recently inherited a sizable estate from her silly humans (who had left all of their possessions to their cat rather than their children). However, Elizabeth could not censure Wickham for his attentions to Miss King, as she understood that sleek, handsome toms must eat as well as those with tattered ears and mournful meows.

"My dearest Lizzy will, I am sure, be incapable of triumphing in her better judgement, at my expense, when I confess myself to have been entirely deceived in Miss Bingley's regard for me. But, my dear sister, though the event has proved you right, do not think me obstinate if I still assert, that, considering what her behaviour was, my confidence was as natural as your suspicion. I do not at all comprehend her reason for wishing to be intimate with me, but if the same circumstances were to happen again, I am sure I should be deceived again. Caroline did not return my visit till yesterday; and not a note,

not a line, did I receive in the mean time. When she did come, it was very evident that she had no pleasure in it; she made a slight, formal apology, for not calling before, said not a word of wishing to see me again, and was in every respect so altered a creature, that when she went away, I was perfectly resolved to continue the acquaintance no longer. I pity, though I cannot help blaming her. She was very wrong in singling me out as she did; I can safely say, that every advance to intimacy began on her side. But I pity her, because she must feel that she has been acting wrong, and because I am very sure that anxiety for her brother is the cause of it. I need not explain myself farther; and though we know this anxiety to be quite needless, yet if she feels it, it will easily account for her behaviour to me; and so deservedly dear as he is to his sister, whatever anxiety she must feel on his behalf, is natural and amiable. I cannot but wonder, however, at her having any such fears now, because, if he had at all cared about me, we must have met long long ago. He knows of my being in town, I am certain, from something she said herself; and yet it would seem by her manner of talking, as if she wanted to persuade herself that he is really partial to Miss Darcy. I cannot understand it. If I were not afraid of judging harshly, I should be almost tempted to say, that there is a strong appearance of duplicity in all this. But I will endeavour to banish every painful thought, and think only of what will make me happy, your affection, and the invariable kindness of my dear uncle and aunt. Let me hear from you very soon. Miss Bingley said something of his never returning to Netherfield again, of giving up the house, but not with any certainty. We had better not mention it. I am extremely glad that you have such pleasant accounts from our friends at Hunsford. Pray go to see them, with Sir William and Maria. I am sure you will be very comfortable there—Yours, etc."

Chapter Four

JANUARY AND FEBRUARY passed away with the Bennet sisters frequently trotting down the muddy lanes to Meryton and back.

As her stay at Hunsford drew near, Elizabeth found herself looking forward to the visit. Kitty and Lydia did nothing but chase after officers or runaway balls, and Mrs. Bennet did little but lament and complain, so a change would be most welcome. (It seemed that Mrs. Bennet had not enough sense to understand that life is not just a pill pocket, but a pill, and a cat must take the bitter with the succulent.)

On the way to Hunsford, Elizabeth, who was traveling with Sir William Lucas and his daughter, Maria, stopped in London to visit Jane and the Gardiners. Though Elizabeth found Jane as fluffy as ever, she was concerned to hear from their aunt that Jane still slept twenty-three hours a day, though she endeavored, in the remaining hour of wakefulness, to support her spirits as best she could.

From Aunt Gardiner, Lizzy received an invitation for a summer outing to the lakes.

"Oh, my dear, dear aunt," Lizzy rapturously cried, "what delight! What felicity! You give me fresh life and vigor. What are young toms to the joy of scampering over rocks and mountains? Oh! What hours of transport we shall spend! And when we do return, it shall not be like other cats, shut up in a cat carrier and mewing under the seat of the carriage. We will know where we have gone—we will recollect what trees we have climbed and what squirrels we have stalked!"

The farewell between [Elizabeth] and Mr. Wickham was perfectly friendly; on his side even more. His present pursuit could not make him forget that Elizabeth had been the first to excite and to deserve his attention, the first to listen and to pity, the first to be admired; and in his manner of bidding her adieu, wishing her every enjoyment, reminding her of what she was to expect in Lady Catherine de Bourgh, and trusting their opinion of her—their opinion of every body—would always coincide, there was a solicitude, an interest which she felt must ever attach her to him with a most sincere regard; and she parted from him convinced, that whether married or single, he must always be her model of the amiable and pleasing.

Amiable and pleasing? You think that if it makes you happy.

At length, Elizabeth and her companions arrived at Hunsford. Charlotte greeted Elizabeth with a quiet but earnest chirp, while Mr. Collins paraded proudly around the house and garden, rolled under the sideboard, and caught a magpie in his meadow as if to make Elizabeth feel all the delights she had forfeited in refusing his paw in marriage. Foremost among the felicities of Hunsford were the attentions of Lady Cat. These Elizabeth was to experience the following evening, as the Hunsford party was invited to dine at Rosings. Indeed, Miss Anne de Bourgh had come herself with her lady companion to deliver the invitation. Elizabeth was amused to see how cross and sickly Miss de Bourgh appeared (the perfect future match for Mr. Darcy). In truth, poor Anne had just been to the vet and been weighed, an experience so frightening that she left half her hair behind in the cat carrier.

At length the Parsonage was discernible. The garden sloping to the road, the house standing in it, the green pales and the laurel hedge, every thing declared they were arriving. Mr. Collins and Charlotte appeared at the door, and the carriage stopped at the small gate, which led by a short gravel walk to the house, amidst the nods and smiles of the whole party. In a moment they were all out of the

chaise, rejoicing at the sight of each other. Mrs. Collins welcomed her friend with the liveliest pleasure, and Elizabeth was more and more satisfied with coming, when she found herself so affectionately received. She saw instantly that her cousin's manners were not altered by his marriage; his formal civility was just what it had been, and he detained her some minutes at the gate to hear and satisfy his enquiries after all her family. They were then, with no other delay than his pointing out the neatness of the entrance, taken into the house; and as soon as they were in the parlour, he welcomed them a second time with ostentatious formality to his humble abode, and punctually repeated all his wife's offers of refreshment.

He welcomed them to his humble abode.

Chapter Six

Mr. Collins was in a state of protracted ecstasy at the thought of displaying Lady Cat's grand house to Elizabeth and the others, as well as his patroness's expensive furniture (her new ottoman was especially well-suited for sharpening his claws on) and superlative dishes. Elizabeth was instructed to anticipate wet food *truly* deserving of the name "Fancy Feast."

Sir William and Maria were nearly overpowered by so much grandeur. When the group arrived at Rosings, Sir William said nothing, but Maria immediately scooted under a sofa so that only her tail and hind paws were visible.

Lady Cat was extraordinarily fond of hearing herself meow.

Elizabeth, however, found herself quite composed in the presence of the grand lady, her daughter, and their richly-furnished house.

Lady Cat was extraordinarily fond of hearing herself meow, and interrogated Elizabeth as to all the particulars of her family and upbringing.

"Your father's estate is entailed on Mr. Collins, I think," she observed.

Mr. Collins opened his mouth to chirp his apologies, but his tail, which waved ostentatiously, told another story. Charlotte, however, with great presence of mind, sat on it.

Lady Cat seemed quite taken aback when Elizabeth declined to give her a direct answer as to her age.

"At least," said that fine lady, "you need not be ashamed to give your age in human years."

"Ah, but Ma'am," replied Elizabeth, "surely you would then divide the number by seven and have your answer."

Lady Cat regarded Elizabeth through narrowed eyes before turning the subject to her great condescension in finding a home for three young cats of her acquaintance. Long did she dwell on her great good deeds and general wonderfulness before ordering her carriage (one of several, as Mr. Collins reminded Elizabeth) to take the Hunsford party home. Maria was still under the chair when the carriage arrived and had to be dragged out by her tail. She protested by mewing loudly—the first sound she had made since entering Rosings.

When the ladies returned to the drawing room, there was little to be done but to hear Lady Catherine talk, which she did without any intermission till coffee came in, delivering her opinion on every subject in so decisive a manner as proved that she was not used to have her judgement controverted. She enquired into Charlotte's domestic concerns familiarly and minutely, and gave her a great deal of advice, as to the management of them all; told her how every thing ought to be regulated in so small a family as her's, and instructed her as to the care of her cows and her poultry. Elizabeth found that nothing was beneath this great Lady's attention, which could furnish

her with an occasion of dictating to others. In the intervals of her discourse with Mrs. Collins, she addressed a variety of questions to Maria and Elizabeth, but especially to the latter, of whose connections she knew the least, and who she observed to Mrs. Collins, was a very genteel, pretty kind of girl. She asked her at different times, how many sisters she had, whether they were older or younger than herself, whether any of them were likely to be married, whether they were handsome, where they had been educated, what carriage her father kept, and what had been her mother's maiden name?—Elizabeth felt all the impertinence of her questions, but answered them very composedly.

Chapter Seven

ALTHOUGH ELIZABETH MARVELED that Charlotte could tolerate the irksome society of Mr. Collins, she soon discovered that he spent the chief of every morning hunting in his garden. His afternoons were spent sprawled on his desk dozing or gazing out of his window in hopes of glimpsing Miss de Bourgh's phaeton. To her credit and sense, Mrs. Collins encouraged her husband in all these activities. Thus, Charlotte spent many hours in contented solitude.

Mr. Collins and Charlotte ambled to Rosings almost every afternoon and were occasionally favored by a visit from Lady Cat herself. This great lady pried into every aspect of Charlotte's domestic arrangements. She poked into every corner, sharpened her claws on the furniture, meowed for refreshment, and then sniffed suspiciously and walked away with her ears back when it was served.

As Easter approached, Mr. Darcy and his cousin, Colonel Fitzwilliam, were expected at Rosings. Elizabeth looked forward to observing Mr. Darcy's behavior towards the sickly Miss de Bourgh, for whom he was destined and who had been throwing up hairballs all week. If, as Lady Cat remarked, it hadn't been for the hairballs, her daughter would have been a picture of feline loveliness and health.

On the day Mr. Darcy and his cousin were to arrive, Mr. Collins paced eagerly back and forth in the lane within view of Rosings. As

This great lady pried into every aspect of Charlotte's domestic arrangements.

soon as he spotted the carriage, he ran home to proclaim the great news of the arrival of these two esteemed cats.

That very afternoon, Mr. Darcy and his cousin came to visit the parsonage, much to Charlotte's amazement.

"I may thank you, Eliza, for this piece of civility. Mr. Darcy would never have come so soon to wait upon me," she said.

Mr. Darcy, however, was as grave and silent as ever. Probably, Elizabeth conjectured, he was recalling her muddy paws when she came to visit the ailing Jane at Netherfield or obsessing about her inferior pedigree.

Colonel Fitzwilliam entered into conversation directly with the readiness and ease of a well-bred man, and talked very pleasantly; but his cousin, after having addressed a slight observation on the house and garden to Mrs. Collins, sat for some time without speaking to any body. At length, however, his civility was so far awakened as to enquire of Elizabeth after the health of her family. She answered him in the usual way, and after a moment's pause, added,

"My eldest sister has been in town these three months. Have you never happened to see her there?"

She was perfectly sensible that he never had; but she wished to see whether he would betray any consciousness of what had passed between the Bingleys and Jane; and she thought he looked a little confused as he answered that he had never been so fortunate as to meet Miss Bennet. The subject was pursued no farther, and the gentlemen soon afterwards went away.

Chapter Eight

Colonel Fitzwilliam made himself most agreeable to all the party at the parsonage, but it was a full week before they received another invitation from Lady Cat to visit Rosings. And then, when they arrived, she greeted them coolly and mainly purred to her two nephews. Colonel Fitzwilliam, however, engaged Elizabeth in chasing a piece of fluff under a chair and the two frolicked with such spirit and flow that Lady Cat insisted on joining them, nearly spoiling their sport.

After catnip tea, Colonel Fitzwilliam reminded Elizabeth of her promise to pounce on the piano, and though Elizabeth acquitted herself with both grace and animation, Lady Cat scolded her for not practicing more and meowed loudly all through Elizabeth's performance.

"How well Anne would have performed," she proclaimed, "if only she had the strength to jump on the keys. I, too, would have been a great proficient," she added, "if I'd made the slightest effort."

While Elizabeth was performing, Mr. Darcy walked magisterially up to the piano, where he could command a full view of Elizabeth who, however, refused to be intimidated. Instead, she playfully exposed Mr. Darcy's true character to Colonel Fitzwilliam by relating how, at a country gathering in Hertfordshire, Darcy refused to chase a feather, though there were many cats willing to romp with him.

**I didn't make a fuss when they threw me out of their bedroom
for a minor indiscretion.**

"I have not the talent," replied Mr. Darcy, in his defense, "which some cats possess of frolicking easily with those I have never encountered before. I cannot catch their easy playfulness or appear interested in their favorite brand of cat food, napping routines, or method of enslaving their owners."

"I, too," replied Elizabeth, "have often fallen short in my ambition to enslave my owners, but then I have always supposed it to be my fault because I didn't make a huge fuss when they threw me out of their bedroom for a minor indiscretion."

"We, neither of us," said Mr. Darcy, gazing deeply into Elizabeth's eyes, "perform well to strangers."

"You mean to frighten me, Mr. Darcy, by coming in all this state to hear me? I will not be alarmed though your sister does *play so well. There is a stubbornness about me that never can bear to be*

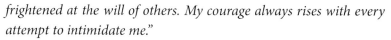

frightened at the will of others. My courage always rises with every attempt to intimidate me."

"I shall not say that you are mistaken," he replied, "because you could not really believe me to entertain any design of alarming you; and I have had the pleasure of your acquaintance long enough to know, that you find great enjoyment in occasionally professing opinions which in fact are not your own."

Elizabeth laughed heartily at this picture of herself, and said to Colonel Fitzwilliam, "Your cousin will give you a very pretty notion of me, and teach you not to believe a word I say. I am particularly unlucky in meeting with a person so well able to expose my real character, in a part of the world where I had hoped to pass myself off with some degree of credit."

. . .

Here they were interrupted by Lady Catherine, who called out to know what they were talking of. Elizabeth immediately began playing again. Lady Catherine approached, and, after listening for a few minutes, said to Darcy,

Anne would have been a delightful performer, had her health allowed her to learn.

"Miss Bennet would not play at all amiss, if she practiced more, and could have the advantage of a London master. She has a very good notion of fingering, though her taste is not equal to Anne's. Anne would have been a delightful performer, had her health allowed her to learn."

Chapter Nine

ELIZABETH WAS CLEANING herself in solitude one morning when she was startled by the entrance of Mr. Darcy. Mr. Darcy, likewise, seemed surprised at finding her alone. However, he promptly sat down and commenced washing his face.

After a little conversation and many long silences, Mr. Darcy commented that Mr. Collins appeared fortunate in his choice of a mate. Elizabeth agreed that, in general, Charlotte was a wise and sensible cat.

"And she is but fifty miles from her home," observed Mr. Darcy. And then, moving closer to Elizabeth, he began to purr. "I think you would not want to be so close to Longbourn always?"

Elizabeth looked surprised. Mr. Darcy seemed to recollect himself and promptly sat down on a newspaper and stared steadfastly into a corner of the room until Charlotte and Maria appeared.

"What can be the meaning of this?" asked Charlotte, as soon as he was gone. "My dear, Eliza, he must be in love with you, or he would never have called on us in this familiar way."

When Elizabeth, however, described Mr. Darcy's long silences, even Charlotte was doubtful.

Perhaps, the two agreed, Mr. Darcy was merely bored, for the field sports were over and he was for the present consigned to being a house cat.

Field sports were over and he was consigned to being a house cat.

It was plain to them all that Colonel Fitzwilliam came because he had pleasure in their society, a persuasion which of course recommended him still more; and Elizabeth was reminded by her own satisfaction in being with him, as well as by his evident admiration of her, of her former favourite George Wickham; and though, in comparing them, she saw there was less captivating softness in Colonel Fitzwilliam's manners, she believed he might have the best informed mind.

But why Mr. Darcy came so often to the Parsonage, it was more difficult to understand. It could not be for society, as he frequently sat there ten minutes together without opening his lips; and when he did speak, it seemed the effect of necessity rather than of choice—a sacri-

97

fice to propriety, not a pleasure to himself. He seldom appeared really animated. Mrs. Collins knew not what to make of him. Colonel Fitz-william's occasionally laughing at his stupidity, proved that he was generally different, which her own knowledge of him could not have told her; and as she would have liked to have believed this change the effect of love, and the object of that love her friend Eliza, she set herself seriously to work to find it out.—She watched him when-ever they were at Rosings, and whenever he came to Hunsford; but without much success. He certainly looked at her friend a great deal, but the expression of that look was disputable. It was an earnest, steadfast gaze, but she often doubted whether there were much admi-ration in it, and sometimes it seemed nothing but absence of mind.

Chapter Ten

ELIZABETH OFTEN ENJOYED prowling around the park while she was at Hunsford. She encountered Mr. Darcy more than once in the wood during these walks, which perplexed her. The circumstance struck her as perverse, even for a cat, because she was perfectly sensible of the fact that Mr. Darcy took little pleasure in her company. Yet he persisted in sniffing the same shrubs she sniffed, climbing the same trees she scampered up to avoid him, even pouncing on the very insects she intended to capture for herself. His curiosity further expressed itself in questions about her home in Hertfordshire, what she thought of Mr. and Mrs. Collins's union, and whether she looked forward to exploring the great rooms of Rosings. Towards what could these questions tend?

On one such a solitary ramble, Elizabeth met not Mr. Darcy, but Colonel Fitzwilliam. He accompanied her back to the parsonage, and in the course of their conversation revealed that Darcy had lately saved a friend from the inconvenience of a most imprudent match by disentangling him from the velvet claws of a "certain country cat." That the friend was Bingley, and the certain "country cat" her sister Jane, Elizabeth could not doubt.

Back in her own room in Hunsford, Elizabeth was so agitated by the pain Mr. Darcy had caused Jane by separating her from Mr. Bingley that she began shedding profusely and was suited by neither humor nor hair to present herself at Rosings. The Hunsford party, thus, went on without her.

During the course of the evening, Elizabeth pondered what Mr. Darcy could have objected to in her sister. She settled the matter by deciding it was nothing more than the Gardiners' residence in Cheapside, and Mr. Gardiner's propensity to hunt rats in his own warehouses in London.

She was engaged one day as she walked, in re-perusing Jane's last letter, and dwelling on some passages which proved that Jane had not written in spirits, when, instead of being again surprised by Mr. Darcy, she saw on looking up that Colonel Fitzwilliam was meeting her.

. . .

"I imagine your cousin brought you down with him chiefly for the sake of having some body at his disposal [said Elizabeth]. *I wonder he does not marry, to secure a lasting convenience of that kind. But, perhaps his sister does as well for the present, and, as she is under his sole care, he may do what he likes with her."*

"No," said Colonel Fitzwilliam, "that is an advantage which he must divide with me. I am joined with him in the guardianship of Miss Darcy."

"Are you indeed? And pray what sort of guardians do you make? Does your charge give you much trouble? Young ladies of her age are sometimes a little difficult to manage, and if she has the true Darcy spirit, she may like to have her own way."

As she spoke, she observed him looking at her earnestly; and the manner in which he immediately asked her why she supposed Miss Darcy likely to give them any uneasiness, convinced her that she had somehow or other got pretty near the truth. She directly replied,

"You need not be frightened. I never heard any harm of her; and I dare say she is one of the most tractable creatures in the world. She is a very great favourite with some ladies of my acquaintance, Mrs. Hurst and Miss Bingley."

Chapter Eleven

WHEN EVERYONE HAD gone, Elizabeth employed herself in batting about Jane's letters (which of course, put her in an even worse humor with Mr. Darcy). Thank goodness he would soon be leaving Rosings!

A moment later, Elizabeth was startled by the sound of the doorbell. She scooted under the couch in an instant, where she always fled when the doorbell rang. (As distressing were her reflections on Jane's heartbreak and Mr. Darcy's heartless*ness*, they were nothing compared to the ringing of a doorbell.) Perhaps, thought Elizabeth, peeking out, it was Colonel Fitzwilliam. But instead, to her amazement, Mr. Darcy, and Mr. Darcy only, walked into the room.

He appeared quite distracted, but catching sight of Elizabeth's tail waving under the couch, thought to inquire after her health. Venturing out of her hiding place, Elizabeth answered coldly and immediately commenced licking her paw.

A long silence followed, during which Mr. Darcy hopped onto a chair, hopped down and then back up again, then began:

"In vain I have struggled. It will not do. My feelings will not be repressed. You must allow me to tell you how ardently I admire and love you."

Elizabeth's astonishment was beyond expression. She stopped licking her paw, stared at him, and was silent.

This Mr. Dar̲ ̲ ̲ ̲ ̲nt encouragement, and he went on with ̲ ̲ ̲ ̲ ̲ ̲ ̲ ̲ ̲ ̲to communicate what he had lon̲ ̲ ̲ ̲ ̲ ̲ ̲ ̲ ̲at not only about his passionate a̲ ̲ ̲ ̲ ̲ ̲ ̲ also dwelt with warmth on all the reason̲ ̲ ̲ ̲ ̲gradation to him by virtue of Elizabeth's comm̲ ̲ ̲ ̲ ̲her mother's side, and inferior connections, partic̲ ̲ ̲r rat-hunting uncle in Cheapside. He made it abundantly clear that if he *could* have resisted her, he certainly would have. But, as he had not been successful in repressing his feelings, he fervently hoped she would put him out of his misery and accept his paw in marriage.

Arching her back, Elizabeth composed herself as best she could. She then made it clear that though she wished she could feel grateful for the honor of his offer, she must refuse him.

Leaping up to the mantle, Mr. Darcy stared at her in disbelief.

"Cat got your tongue?" asked Elizabeth archly.

Darcy recollected himself. "And this is all the reply which I am to have the honor of expecting?! I might, perhaps, wish to be informed why, with so little endeavor at civility, I am thus rejected."

"And I," replied Elizabeth, "might as well inquire why, with so evident a design of offending and insulting me, you chose to tell me that your regard for me rubbed your fur the wrong way! And what about the unhappiness you caused my dear sister Jane by separating her from Mr. Bingley?"

Mr. Darcy did not deny it.

"And the injuries you inflicted on poor Wickham?" went on Elizabeth.

"His injuries!" snarled Mr. Darcy. "Oh, it was a cat-fight indeed. But Wickham has no injuries to resent."

"You have deprived him of at least six of his nine lives, and of that independence which is both the will and wish of every cat."

"And this," Mr. Darcy said after a pause, "is your opinion of me?"

Elizabeth hissed.

A moment later, mortified and ashamed by what his feelings had been, and by Elizabeth's censure and scorn, Mr. Darcy hastily quit the room.

The scene left Elizabeth in a pitiful state. When she thought of all that had just passed between Mr. Darcy and herself, the confusion and tumult of her mind was great. A moment later, she heard Lady Cat's carriage in the lane, and reflecting how little able she was to present herself to Charlotte's scrutiny, she hastily retreated upstairs to her room, her ears flattened against her head.

"Could you expect me to rejoice in the inferiority of your connections?" [said Darcy] *"To congratulate myself on the hope of relations, whose condition in life is so decidedly beneath my own?"*

Elizabeth felt herself growing more angry every moment; yet she tried to the utmost to speak with composure when she said,

"You are mistaken, Mr. Darcy, if you suppose that the mode of your declaration affected me in any other way, than as it spared the concern which I might have felt in refusing you, had you behaved in a more gentleman-like manner."

She saw him start at this, but he said nothing, and she continued,

"You could not have made the offer of your hand in any possible way that would have tempted me to accept it."

Again his astonishment was obvious; and he looked at her with an expression of mingled incredulity and mortification. She went on.

"From the very beginning, from the first moment I may almost say, of my acquaintance with you, your manners impressing me with the fullest belief of your arrogance, your conceit, and your selfish disdain of the feelings of others, were such as to form that groundwork of disapprobation, on which succeeding events have built so immoveable a dislike; and I had not known you a month before I

felt that you were the last man in the world whom I could ever be prevailed on to marry."

Chapter Twelve

THE NEXT MORNING, feeling unequal to indoor employment, Elizabeth resolved to indulge in air and exercise, and set off directly after breakfast. She had just paused to look into the park and nibble a tender blade of grass when she glimpsed Mr. Darcy himself coming towards her. Before she could flee, he called her name and placed a letter in her paw. Then he withdrew and was soon out of sight.

It was a very fat letter, and Elizabeth took pleasure in rolling around and kicking it with her back paws, until she settled down to peruse its contents.

In the letter, Mr. Darcy addressed at length the two things Elizabeth had charged him with: separating Mr. Bingley from her sister Jane and ruining at least six of Wickham's nine lives, leaving him but three to limp by on.

In alluding to his conduct with Mr. Bingley, Darcy professed that the mild-mannered Jane was so composed that no one who observed her closely could think her deeply attached to Bingley, though Bingley was obviously attached to her. His attachment was cause for alarm for both himself and the Bingley sisters, he went on to explain. Their anxieties were raised not only by Jane's inferior cat connections, but by the improper and impudent behavior exhibited by the three youngest Bennet cats, their mother, and occasionally even Mr. Bennet. Darcy confessed he had colluded in concealing Jane's presence in London to ensure that his friend remained safe from either pettings or purrs involving Miss Bennet.

Mr. Darcy then went on to elucidate the whole of the painful history between Mr. Wickham and himself. Not only had Wickham deceived old Mr. Darcy as to the true nature of his character (including a vicious propensity to bite and certain indelicate behaviors involving female cats), he had even attempted to run away with Georgiana Darcy, a plan that Mr. Darcy had fortuitously frustrated before Wickham could carry it out. Since then, Wickham's life had been one of idleness and dissipation, one lower and more depraved than that of the most indulged house cat.

"This, madam," ended Mr. Darcy, "is a faithful narrative of every event in which we have been concerned together; and if you do not absolutely reject it as false, you will, I hope, acquit me henceforth of cruelty towards Mr. Wickham."

Wickham's life had been one of idleness and dissipation.

"You may possibly wonder why all this was not told you last night. But I was not then master enough of myself to know what could or ought to be revealed. For the truth of everything here related, I can appeal more particularly to the testimony of Colonel Fitzwilliam, who from our near relationship and constant intimacy, and, still more as one of the executors of my father's will, has been unavoidably acquainted with every particular of these transactions. If your abhorrence of me *should make* my *assertions valueless*, you cannot be prevented by the same cause from confiding in my cousin; and that there may be the possibility of consulting him, I shall endeavour to find some opportunity of putting this letter in your hands in the course of the morning. I will only add, God bless you.

"FITZWILLIAM DARCY"

Chapter Thirteen

AFTER HER FIRST perusal of Mr. Darcy's letter, Elizabeth derived an almost perverse pleasure in biting and clawing it. As she had suspected, it had no fresh intelligence to communicate that would clear Mr. Darcy of cruelty in separating her sister from Mr. Bingley, or of his unfeeling and infamous behavior towards Mr. Wickham. But when she paused and scanned the letter more closely (and she had a strong suspicion that he had sprinkled it with catnip to assure repeated readings), she realized that, in regard to Mr. Wickham, she had no actual knowledge of his history or character but what Wickham himself had related to her. Wickham was such a fine, handsome specimen that everyone in Meryton had been captivated by his grace and good looks and no one had doubted that he was one of the most upstanding cats in the country. Elizabeth recalled how he had said he could never attack Mr. Darcy (or his character) out of his respect for the late Mr. Darcy. Yet as soon as Darcy and the Bingleys removed from Netherfield, Wickham had done exactly that. How painful it was to think that she, Elizabeth, had been so partial, prejudiced, and willfully blind!

In regard to her sister and Bingley, Elizabeth crouched in shame under a laurel hedge when she recalled the inappropriate behavior of her parents and younger sisters on the occasion of Mr. Bingley's procuring that splendid ball. Lydia especially (who had been in heat) had chased the officers most recklessly and Mrs. Bennet had boasted to Lady Lucas of Jane's imminent union with Mr. Bingley.

Back at Hunsford, Elizabeth learned that both Mr. Darcy and Colonel Fitzwilliam had called to take their leave during her absence. Elizabeth was not sorry to have missed them. She could now think only of her letter and trotted upstairs to her room with it in her mouth.

Whether or not Mr. Darcy had, in fact, scented it with catnip was uncertain. But, catnip or not, the truth of what he had communicated was indisputable.

The extravagance and general profligacy which [Darcy] *scrupled not to lay to Mr. Wickham's charge, exceedingly shocked her; the more so, as she could bring no proof of its injustice. She had never heard of him before his entrance into the _____shire Militia, in which he had engaged at the persuasion of the young man, who, on meeting him accidentally in town, had there renewed a slight acquaintance. Of his former way of life, nothing had been known in Hertfordshire but what he told himself. As to his real character, had information been in her power, she had never felt a wish of enquiring. His countenance, voice, and manner, had established him at once in the possession of every virtue. She tried to recollect some instance of goodness, some distinguished trait of integrity or benevolence, that might rescue him from the attacks of Mr. Darcy; or at least, by the predominance of virtue, atone for those casual errors, under which she would endeavour to class what Mr. Darcy had described as the idleness and vice of many years continuance. But no such recollection befriended her. She could see him instantly before her, in every charm of air and*

address; but she could remember no more substantial good than the general approbation of the neighbourhood, and the regard which his social powers had gained him in the mess.

LADY CAT WAS rendered so dull and dispirited by the departure of her nephews that she invited the Hunsford party to dine with her that night. Smiling to herself, Elizabeth reflected that had she accepted Mr. Darcy's proposal, she—Elizabeth, descendant of a common cat on her mother's side—might by now have been introduced to Lady Cat as her future niece!

Lady Cat urged Elizabeth with more persistence than politeness to extend her stay in Hunsford, but when Elizabeth declined, her ladyship contented herself with reminding Lizzy of the advisability of traveling with a veterinarian (as she invariably did with Anne), dictating the manner in which she was to pad her cat carrier, and finally condescending to wish her and Maria a good journey and invite them to visit Hunsford again the following year.

The two gentlemen left Rosings the next morning; and Mr. Collins having been in waiting near the lodges, to make them his parting obeisance, was able to bring home the pleasing intelligence, of their appearing in very good health, and in as tolerable spirits as could be expected, after the melancholy scene so lately gone through at Rosings. To Rosings he then hastened to console Lady Catherine and her daughter; and on his return, brought back, with great satisfaction, a message from her Ladyship, importing that she felt herself

so dull as to make her very desirous of having them all to dine with her.

Elizabeth could not see Lady Catherine without recollecting that, had she chosen it, she might by this time have been presented to her, as her future niece; nor could she think, without a smile, of what her ladyship's indignation would have been. "What would she have said?– how would she have behaved?" were questions with which she amused herself.

Their first subject was the diminution of the Rosings party. "I assure you, I feel it exceedingly," said Lady Catherine; "I believe no body feels the loss of friends so much as I do. But I am particularly attached to these young men; and know them to be so much attached to me!—They were excessively sorry to go! But so they always are. The dear colonel rallied his spirits tolerably till just at last; but Darcy seemed to feel it most acutely, more I think than last year. His attach-ment to Rosings certainly increases."

<hr />

I just want to see what happens at the end.

Chapter Fifteen

ON THE MORNING Elizabeth and Maria were to leave Hunsford, Mr. Collins attacked Elizabeth over breakfast with protracted civilities and gratitude for her condescension in visiting them.

"How dull it must have been for you here, my dear cousin," said he, "with our small rooms, solitary hours, and few humans (though I flatter myself that may be an advantage). However," he went on, "you have been so fortunate as to dine frequently at Rosings."

Words were insufficient for the elevation of his feelings; and he was obliged to walk about the room. Elizabeth stifled a yawn and tried to look attentive.

"No one who knows our intimacy with Lady Cat can think us unfortunate," Mr. Collins went on after a moment. "My dear Charlotte and I trot over there nearly every day. You see what footing we're on!" he cried, ostentatiously grooming himself. "How fortunate an alliance your friend has made."

Elizabeth assented to all he said. But to herself she thought: *Poor Charlotte! It was melancholy indeed, to leave her to such society.* But Charlotte appeared tolerably cheerful. Her home, her humans, her poultry, and her prey had not lost their charms.

Maria and Elizabeth soon boarded the carriage and curled up under the seat. Elizabeth looked forward with pleasure to seeing her aunt and uncle in London, and especially her sister, Jane. How much she would have to tell her, she thought as the carriage wheels rumbled along. And how much she would have to conceal.

If she could only determine which was which!

"It gives me the greatest pleasure [said Mr. Collins] *to hear that you have passed your time not disagreeably. We have certainly done our best; and most fortunately having it in our power to introduce you to very superior society, and from our connection with Rosings, the frequent means of varying the humble home scene, I think we may flatter ourselves that your Hunsford visit cannot have been entirely irksome. Our situation with regard to Lady Catherine's family is indeed the sort of extraordinary advantage and blessing which few can boast. You see on what a footing we are. You see how continually we are engaged there. In truth I must acknowledge that, with all the disadvantages of this humble parsonage, I should not think anyone abiding in it an object of compassion, while they are sharers of our intimacy at Rosings."*

Words were insufficient for the elevation of his feelings; and he was obliged to walk about the room, while Elizabeth tried to unite civility with truth in a few short sentences.

"You may, in fact, carry a very favourable report of us into Hert-fordshire, my dear cousin. I flatter myself at least that you will be able to do so. Lady Catherine's great attentions to Mrs. Collins you have been a daily witness of, and altogether I trust it does not appear that your friend has drawn an unfortunate—but on this point it will be as well to be silent. Only let me assure you, my dear Miss Eliza-beth, that I can from my heart most cordially wish you equal felicity in marriage. My dear Charlotte and I have but one mind and one

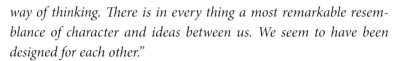

way of thinking. *There is in every thing a most remarkable resemblance of character and ideas between us. We seem to have been designed for each other.*"

Chapter Sixteen

In May, Elizabeth, Jane, and Maria left London for Longbourn (without a veterinarian, in spite of Lady Cat's advice and admonitions). When they changed carriages, they were surprised to find Lydia and Kitty waiting for them at the inn. They had been waiting for an hour, during which they occupied themselves arranging cold meats and crunchies and attacking a bonnet.

"I intend to destroy it completely when we get home," Lydia announced. "I dare say it will look better torn to pieces. Anyway," she added, looking dejected, "it doesn't signify whether our bonnets are in pieces or not, for the militia are leaving Meryton and going to Brighton."

Thank goodness! thought Elizabeth. *Perhaps Kitty and Lydia will stop chasing all the cats in the militia and settle down!*

"The militia is to be encamped near Brighton," continued Lydia, "and I do so want papa to take us all there for the summer!"

Elizabeth shuddered at the thought of Lydia with an entire camp full of toms when one poor militia and a few balls had driven all sense (what little she had) out of her head.

"Now I have got some news about a cat we all admire," said Lydia, as they crouched down at the table.

Elizabeth told the waiter he need not stay.

"As if the waiter cares what I am going to communicate!" scoffed Lydia. "But he is a scrawny cat; I never saw such ridiculously long whiskers in my life."

Lydia went on to relate that Mary King, whom Wickham had lately been forming designs on, had left Meryton. Wickham was a free cat again.

Jane looked concerned. "I hope there was no strong attachment between the two," she ventured.

"Oh," said Lydia carelessly, "I will answer for it; he never cared three straws for her—who could about such an ugly spotted thing?"

Soon afterward, the four Bennet sisters and Maria crammed themselves into the carriage with their cat carriers, ribbons, and remnants of Lydia's new bonnet.

"Dear me!" cried Lydia as they rattled along. "What a good piece of fun we had the other day at Colonel Forster's. What do

Who could care about such an ugly spotted thing?

Lord, how funny he looked and how we laughed!

you think we did? We dressed up Chamberlayne to pass for a lady. Lord, how funny he looked and how we laughed!"

They came home to a warm welcome and a big family party at dinner. Lydia gaily described the fun and noise of being crowded together in the carriage.

"I was ready to die of laughter!" she said.

Mary just looked sour. "I should infinitely prefer a book," she replied.

In the afternoon Lydia was urgent with the rest of the girls to walk to Meryton and to see how every body went on; but Elizabeth steadily opposed the scheme. It should not be said, that the Miss Bennets could not be at home half a day before they were in pursuit

of the officers. There was another reason too for her opposition. She dreaded seeing Wickham again, and was resolved to avoid it as long as possible. The comfort to her, of the regiment's approaching removal, was indeed beyond expression. In a fortnight they were to go, and once gone, she hoped there could be nothing more to plague her on his account.

ELIZABETH WAS IMPATIENT to relate to Jane all that had passed at Hunsford between herself and Mr. Darcy—excepting, of course, Mr. Darcy's role in separating Bingley from Jane. That intelligence could only give her sister pain.

Jane was at first astonished to hear of Mr. Darcy's proposal, and grieved that he should be suffering any pain from Elizabeth's refusal. But this was nothing compared to her sister's dismay on learning that Wickham was as wanton and wicked as a wild dog. Jane would have liked to believe that no such wickedness existed in all the world as was here collected in one cat!

"Poor Wickham!" cried Jane. "There is such an expression of goodness in his soft blinks! Such an openness and gentleness in his manner of purring."

"There certainly was some great mismanagement in the upbringing of those two cats," Elizabeth replied. "One has got all the goodness, and the other all the appearance of it."

The two sisters discussed whether they should make their knowledge of Wickham's true character public.

Elizabeth thought it should not be attempted.

"You are quite right," said Jane. "He is now, perhaps, sorry for what he has done, and anxious to reestablish a character. We must not make him desperate. He might, perhaps, be driven into the sewers of London to live a life of decadence and debauchery."

One has got all the goodness and the other all the appearance of goodness.

Meanwhile, Mrs. Bennet continued to fuss and fret over Mr. Bingley's leaving Netherfield, not realizing how much pain her incessant complaining gave Jane.

"To think he has escaped and now nothing will come of their attachment which seemed so promising only a few short months ago!" she wailed.

"Well, Lizzy," she continued soon afterwards, "and so the Collinses live very comfortably, do they? Charlotte is an excellent manager, I dare say, and catches plenty of rodents and makes them go a long way. And so I suppose they purr together at the thought of having Longbourn when your father is dead. How unfeeling of them! Well, if they can be easy with an estate that is not lawfully their own, so much the better. I should be ashamed of having one that was only end-tailed on me."

⚜

"Well, Lizzy," said Mrs. Bennet one day, "what is your opinion now of this sad business of Jane's? For my part, I am determined *never to speak of it again to anybody. I told my sister Philips so the other day. But I cannot find out that Jane saw any thing of him in London. Well, he is a very undeserving young man–and I do not suppose there is the least chance in the world of her ever getting him now. There is no talk of his coming to Netherfield again in the summer; and I have enquired of every body too, who is likely to know."*

"I do not believe that he will ever live at Netherfield any more."

"Oh well! it is just as he chooses. Nobody wants him to come. Though I shall always say that he used my daughter extremely ill; and if I was her, I would not have put up with it. Well, my comfort is, I am sure Jane will die of a broken heart, and then he will be sorry for what he has done."

Chapter Eighteen

THE DEPARTURE OF the militia from Meryton was now almost at hand. Dejected and disappointed, Lydia and Kitty went completely off their wet food and prowled around the house day and night lamenting their misfortune in losing the society of so many handsome toms. Only Elizabeth and Jane continued to eat, sleep, and play with tolerable composure.

Mrs. Bennet also repined at the perverse turn of events, exacerbated by Mr. Bennet's refusal to take them all to Brighton. "A little sea-bathing would set me up forever," she exclaimed.

Elizabeth felt ashamed of her mother and sisters and was newly sensible of the justice of Mr. Darcy's objections to her family.

Whilst all this was taking place, Lydia's prospects suddenly brightened when she received an invitation from Mrs. Forster, the wife of the Colonel of the regiment, to accompany them to Brighton. At this news, the wild exuberance of Lydia, the delight of their mother, and the agony of Kitty were scarcely to be described.

Elizabeth was so concerned about the danger of Lydia being let loose with hundreds of toms on the beaches of Brighton that she determined to caution her father against letting her go.

"Lydia will never be happy until she has exposed herself in some public place or other," said her father. "We'll have no peace at Longbourn unless she goes."

Elizabeth shook her head. "If you, my dear father, will not take the trouble of teaching her that her present pursuits are not to be the business of her life, her character will be fixed, and she will, at sixteen (an old maid in human years, I might add), be the silliest feline fatale that ever made herself or her family ridiculous."

"At Brighton she will be of less importance even as a common cat than she has been here," replied her father. "At any rate, she cannot grow many degrees worse, without authorizing us to board her for the rest of her life."

In Lydia's imagination, the dazzling prospect of Brighton afforded every possibility of earthly pleasure . . . she saw the beaches crowded with sleek, handsome toms (shaking their back paws when a wave accidentally reached them). She saw all the glories of the camp and, to complete the view, she saw herself the center of attention, cavorting with at least six toms at once.

Before Lydia left, Elizabeth saw Wickham for the last time. He came trotting in, expecting Elizabeth to roll on her back in ecstasy now that he'd lost Mary King, but Elizabeth was disgusted by his attentions and merely flicked her tail and turned away to stare at an invisible spot on the wall.

When the party broke up, Lydia returned with Mrs. Forster to Meryton in preparation to start out for Brighton the next day. The unfortunate Kitty wailed inconsolably on the parting, which was generally so noisy that Lydia failed to hear the more gentle mews of her two older sisters.

❧

On the very last day of the regiment's remaining in Meryton, [Wickham] *dined with others of the officers, at Longbourn; and so little was Elizabeth disposed to part from him in good humour, that*

It's not fair; I want to go to Brighton, too!

on his making some enquiry as to the manner in which her time had passed at Hunsford, she mentioned Colonel Fitzwilliam's and Mr. Darcy's having both spent three weeks at Rosings, and asked him if he were acquainted with the former.

He looked surprised, displeased, alarmed; but with a moment's recollection and a returning smile, replied, that he had formerly seen him often; and after observing that he was a very gentlemanlike man, asked her how she had liked him. Her answer was warmly in his favour. With an air of indifference he soon afterwards added, "How long did you say that he was at Rosings?"

"Nearly three weeks."

"And you saw him frequently?"

"Yes, almost every day."

"His manners are very different from his cousin's."

127

"Yes, very different. But I think Mr. Darcy improves upon acquaintance."

"Indeed!" cried Mr. Wickham with a look which did not escape her. "And pray, may I ask?" but checking himself, he added in a gayer tone, "Is it in address that he improves? Has he deigned to add ought of civility to his ordinary style? for I dare not hope," he continued in a lower and more serious tone, "that he is improved in essentials."

"Oh, no!" said Elizabeth. "In essentials, I believe, he is very much what he ever was."

While she spoke, Wickham looked as if scarcely knowing whether to rejoice over her words, or to distrust their meaning.

Chapter Nineteen

ELIZABETH KNEW THERE was nothing Mr. Bennet (or indeed anyone) could do to enlarge the mind of poor Mrs. Bennet. But Elizabeth earnestly regretted that her father had not preserved the respectability of his daughters and endeavored to check Lydia's wild animal spirits. The impudent behavior of Lydia, Kitty, and Mrs. Bennet must expose the entire family to censure and ridicule and materially damage Elizabeth and Jane's chances of making a good match. However, Lizzy was not disposed to dwell on gloomy prognostications, so she bent her thoughts towards the tour of the lakes with her aunt and uncle.

Lydia had promised to write often, but her letters were infrequent and communicated little aside from a careless claw mark or a hastily nibbled page. And although Kitty appeared to have fuller intelligence, she always carried *her* letters upstairs in her mouth and chewed over their contents under her bed.

As the time approached for Aunt and Uncle Gardiner to arrive, Elizabeth received a letter from her aunt informing her that they would not have time to tour the lakes, and must content themselves with only exploring the beauties of Derbyshire. Mrs. Gardiner was particularly looking forward to visiting the town of Lambton, where she had grown up as a kitten.

Elizabeth could not hear of Derbyshire without thinking of Pemberley, Mr. Darcy's magnificent estate. *But surely*, she thought,

Kitty carried *her* letters upstairs in her mouth and chewed over their contents under her bed.

I may venture into the county and rob it of a few spiders without drawing his notice.

The Gardiners soon arrived with their four kittens, who were to stay at Longbourn while Elizabeth and her aunt and uncle set off on their pleasure trip.

Over the next week or two, the travelers passed through many remarkable towns, most notably Kennelworth (just the place, thought Elizabeth, to send Lydia if she misbehaved at Brighton).

As they neared the home of Mrs. Gardiner's kittenhood, Elizabeth learned that Pemberley was but five miles away.

"I would so like to visit Pemberley, of all things," said Mrs. Gardiner. "You, too, my love," she said to Elizabeth, "must be anxious to see a place you've heard talked of so much. Wickham passed all his youth there."

Elizabeth stared wide-eyed at her aunt. What should she do? She certainly had no business sniffing around Pemberley after what had passed between her and its master. Mr. Darcy might even pick up her scent! But after inquiring at the inn and learning that Darcy and his sister were not at Pemberley for the summer, she declared herself willing enough to visit the great estate.

To Pemberley, therefore, they were to go.

Elizabeth . . . felt that she had no business at Pemberley, and was obliged to assume a disinclination for seeing it. She must own that she was tired of great houses; after going over so many, she really had no pleasure in fine carpets or satin curtains.

Mrs. Gardiner abused her stupidity. "If it were merely a fine house richly furnished," said she, "I should not care about it myself; but the grounds are delightful. They have some of the finest woods in the country."

131

Chapter One

As THEY TURNED in at the lodge at Pemberley, Elizabeth jumped up on the carriage box to get a better view of the prospect before her. The woods were broad and lush; how she longed to get out for a good scratch in the dirt! But a moment later her attention was arrested by the house itself—a large, splendid dwelling on rising ground. She noticed with pleasure that the valleys, woods, and hills surrounding it were unspoiled by human improvement (or what humans call "improvement"). All was artless and natural. At that moment Elizabeth could not help reflecting that to be mistress of Pemberley would really be something!

The housekeeper was a respectable elderly cat who invited them in and gave them a tour of the house, which, Elizabeth noted with admiration, had more elegance and less ostentatious splendor than Rosings. Even the scratching posts showed more real taste (and also more use) than those at Rosings. Elizabeth supposed that was because Lady Cat preferred to use Charlotte Lucas, or whoever else might be at hand, to sharpen her claws on.

Her aunt called Elizabeth to look at a picture. Elizabeth approached and saw a handsome likeness of the whiskered Wickham.

"Ah," said the housekeeper, "that is Mr. Wickham, the son of my late master's top mouser. He is now gone into the army," she added. "But I am afraid he has turned out very wild."

I am afraid he has turned out very wild.

In contrast, the housekeeper purred audibly when she described Mr. Darcy's virtues—his generosity with cats of lesser territory, his affection for his sister, and his kindness to every cat in his employ. This was praise indeed and placed him in a very amiable light.

"This account of Mr. Darcy," her aunt whispered to her, "is not consistent with his behavior to poor Wickham."

"Perhaps we may have been deceived," replied Elizabeth.

The housekeeper pointed out with pride a window perch that Mr. Darcy had fitted up especially for his sister. And in the picture gallery, Elizabeth beheld a portrait of Mr. Darcy and gazed up at the handsome face in earnest contemplation. She had never felt so warmly towards the original as she did at that moment. Whether it was the catnip the housekeeper offered the guests that made her roll on the carpet, or the gratitude she felt when she thought of Mr. Darcy's former regard for her, she could not tell.

When they had looked over the house, Elizabeth and the Gardiners slipped out the back door to explore the grounds. They were ambling across the broad lawn towards the river, when the master himself appeared not twenty yards away.

For a moment both Elizabeth and Darcy stood perfectly still, staring at each other. Darcy blinked first. Then, much to Elizabeth's surprise, he greeted her and made himself most agreeable. His manner, his meows, even his arrogance seemed to have softened since their encounter at Hunsford. Elizabeth hardly knew what to attribute it to! He asked to be introduced to her aunt and uncle and they touched noses very graciously. Was this really the same Mr. Darcy who had asked for her paw in marriage with so little civility and so much insolent pride?

What can it mean? wondered Elizabeth. *Is it possible that he should still love me?*

Mr. Darcy trotted along beside her as they explored the grounds. He told Elizabeth of the Bingleys' and Georgiana's expected arrival at Pemberley the next day. He wished particularly to have the honor of introducing her to his sister.

They stood together on the lawn, waiting for Elizabeth's aunt and uncle who were walking more slowly (Mr. Gardiner having stopped, at Mr. Darcy's invitation, to snag a small fish in the pond). The silence becoming awkward, Elizabeth talked of Cheshire and Kennelworth, of catching moles and chasing squirrels.

The visit ended with the utmost cordiality and a lively curiosity on Elizabeth's side to meet the sister of whom she had heard so much.

In the gallery there were many family portraits, but they could have little to fix the attention of a stranger. Elizabeth walked in quest of the only face whose features would be known to her. At last it arrested her—and she beheld a striking resemblance to Mr. Darcy, with such a smile over the face, as she remembered to have some-

times seen, when he looked at her. She stood several minutes before the picture in earnest contemplation, and returned to it again before they quitted the gallery. Mrs. Reynolds informed them, that it had been taken in his father's lifetime.

There was certainly at this moment, in Elizabeth's mind, a more gentle sensation towards the original, than she had ever felt in the height of their acquaintance. The commendation bestowed on him by Mrs. Reynolds was of no trifling nature. What praise is more valuable than the praise of an intelligent servant? As a brother, a landlord, a master, she considered how many people's happiness were in his guardianship!—How much of pleasure or pain was it in his power to bestow!—how much of good or evil must be done by him!

Mr. Darcy, with such a smile as she remembered to have sometimes seen when he looked at her.

Chapter Two

MR. DARCY AND his sister, Georgiana, visited Elizabeth at the inn the very next day. Elizabeth was at first so discomposed by the sound of the curricle driving up the street that she began energetically scratching a table leg. But immediately recollecting herself, she arranged herself with her front paws neatly together and greeted their visitors with composure.

Mr. Darcy and his sister calling so promptly after Georgiana's arrival at Pemberley, and Elizabeth's initial discomfiture, gave rise in Mr. and Mrs. Gardiners' minds to very new ideas. There was no other explanation for such attentions but that Mr. Darcy was attached to their niece.

Introductions were made. To Elizabeth's surprise, Miss Darcy was not proud as she had heard, but merely shy, for she hid under the sofa almost immediately and peeked out only when she was sure that no one was looking. When her brother did finally coax her out, Elizabeth found her to be of a very sweet and gentle disposition.

Shortly afterward, Mr. Bingley entered the room. He appeared overjoyed at meeting Elizabeth again and scarcely seemed able to refrain from leaping straight up into the air. He asked eagerly after her family, and recalled with real regret how long it had been since he had procured the splendid ball at Netherfield, and watching

Miss Darcy peeked out only when she saw that no one was looking.

him, Elizabeth fancied he was remembering the happy times he had spent rolling it around the room with Jane.

Mr. Darcy looked highly gratified while all this was going on, and Elizabeth was newly astonished by his chirrups and soft blinks in contrast to his haughty demeanor at Netherfield and Rosings. When Elizabeth accepted his sister's invitation to dine at Pemberley, he actually rubbed up against a table leg, purring.

That night, Elizabeth paced around her bedroom trying to understand her feelings for Mr. Darcy. That, after she had rejected his proposal so disdainfully, he was now bent on making himself gracious and agreeable, must be attributed to love, ardent love! Every female cat in the kingdom was scratching at his door (with the exception of Anne de Bourgh, who would have scratched better than anyone *if* she had not been so sickly), and yet he was bent on pleasing *her*. These conjectures chased sleep—and a few frightened mice—entirely away.

He who, she had been persuaded, would avoid her as his greatest enemy, seemed, on this accidental meeting, most eager to preserve the acquaintance, and without any indelicate display of regard, or any peculiarity of manner, where their two selves only were concerned, was soliciting the good opinion of her friends, and bent on making her known to his sister. Such a change in a man of so much pride, excited not only astonishment but gratitude—for to love, ardent love, it must be attributed; and as such its impression on her was of a sort to be encouraged, as by no means unpleasing, though it could not be exactly defined. She respected, she esteemed, she was grateful to him, she felt a real interest in his welfare; and she only wanted to know how far she wished that welfare to depend upon herself, and how far it would be for the happiness of both that she should employ the power, which her fancy told her she still possessed, of bringing on the renewal of his addresses.

What do you mean, there's no such book as *Purr and Petulance*? I heard it was a classic.

Chapter Three

ELIZABETH AND HER aunt and uncle had formed a plan of calling on Miss Darcy the following morning. Upon scampering out of the carriage, Elizabeth could not help wondering how her appearance at Pemberley would be received by Caroline Bingley, whose dislike of her was surely founded on jealousy.

But even Elizabeth could not have anticipated the reaction of the female cats sitting in the saloon, with its magnificent views of woods and hills. Miss Darcy immediately disappeared behind a chair, while Caroline arched her back and actually spit at Elizabeth. With some prompting from Mrs. Annesley, the cat who Georgiana had lived with when in town, she ventured out and offered her guests wet and dry food in a gracious, though retiring, manner.

Caroline Bingley continued to glare at Elizabeth and hissed at her if she happened to draw too close. After Mr. Darcy joined them, she actually took a swipe at her rival by venturing a snide comment regarding Wickham's militia leaving Meryton.

"That must have been a great loss to *your* family," snarled Miss Bingley, hoping to discompose Elizabeth. The maneuver did not succeed, however, and Elizabeth's composure in repelling the attack seemed to give Mr. Darcy fresh satisfaction, for he gazed at her deeply and blinked softly as if they were the only two cats in the room. This provoked Caroline sorely. As soon as the guests had departed, she began abusing Elizabeth behind her back.

Miss Bingley took a swipe at her rival.

"How thin and sickly Eliza Bennet looked this morning," she said. "Her fur was all matted and did you see her paw pads when she leapt on the couch? So rough and coarse!"

"Not surprising," commented Mr. Darcy, "considering she's a great walker."

"For my own part," continued Miss Bingley, "I must confess that I never could see any beauty in her. Her coat is not at all brilliant, her teeth are full of tartar, and her eyes, which have been called so fine, have a sharp, shrewish look. In her air altogether there is a kind of sneakiness that gives cats a bad name."

Mr. Darcy remained silent.

Caroline ought to have remained silent herself, but her jealousy made her reckless. She went on, "I particularly recollect your saying one night, Mr. Darcy, after the Bennets had been dining at

Netherfield, 'She? A beauty?!—I should as soon call her mother a purebred!'"

"Yes," Mr. Darcy hissed sharply, "but that was only when I first saw her, for it is many months since I have considered her as one of the handsomest cats in the country."

He then went away and Miss Bingley was left to all the satisfaction of having forced him to say what gave no one any pain but herself. Indeed, she would have preferred a shot from the vet to the sting of Mr. Darcy's words.

Elizabeth soon saw that she was herself closely watched by Miss Bingley, and that she could not speak a word, especially to Miss Darcy, without calling her attention. This observation would not have prevented her from trying to talk to the latter, had they not been seated at an inconvenient distance; but she was not sorry to be spared the necessity of saying much. Her own thoughts were employing her. She expected every moment that some of the gentlemen would enter the room. She wished, she feared that the master of the house might be amongst them; and whether she wished or feared it most, she could scarcely determine.

. . .

While thus engaged, Elizabeth had a fair opportunity of deciding whether she most feared or wished for the appearance of Mr. Darcy, by the feelings which prevailed on his entering the room; and then, though but a moment before she had believed her wishes to predominate, she began to regret that he came.

Chapter Four

ELIZABETH HAD BEEN disappointed during their visit to Derbyshire not to have received any letters from Jane. But she was rewarded on the third day of their stay by two fat letters from her sister. The first began with an account of balls (especially a knitted one acquired by Mrs. Philips, which had fresh catnip inside), bird hunts, and other delightful summer schemes. But the second letter contained intelligence of an alarming nature.

An express had come to Longbourn at midnight the night before, with news that Lydia had run away, had thrown herself utterly into the claws of—Wickham! They had not gone to Gretna

An express came at midnight.

143

Green, where they might have frolicked respectably, but were thought instead to be hiding in London!

Poor Mrs. Bennet, imagining wild dogs, dark alleys, and all manner of dangers befalling her beloved kitten, had gone into hysterics upon hearing the dreadful news and taken to her bed (the covered one, where she felt safest).

"My father has gone off to London to recover Lydia," wrote Jane, "and my mother is terrified lest Mr. Bennet and Wickham get into a cat fight, and Wickham attack him with a fatal bite!"

Jane concluded her letter by urging Elizabeth and the Gardiners to hurry home as soon as possible, as they were all in a terrible uproar, and Mrs. Bennet screeched and howled from morning until night.

Elizabeth was about to run out in pursuit of her aunt and uncle when the door opened and who should walk into the room but Mr. Darcy!

He looked startled at seeing her agitation, for Elizabeth was trembling more violently than she had when a strange human once picked her up whilst she was rambling on a country lane near Longbourn.

Mr. Darcy looked at her with deep concern.

"I must go at once to find my aunt and uncle!" cried Elizabeth.

"You are not well enough to go!" said Darcy. "Let me get the servant. May I fetch you a bowl of milk for your present relief?"

After a servant had been sent for her aunt and uncle, Elizabeth related the dreadful news of Lydia and Wickham.

"They are gone," she cried, "and Lydia is lost to her friends and family forever—concealed no doubt, in the shadowy corners of London with that whiskered menace, Wickham. Oh, if only I had communicated to my family what he really was! It is entirely my fault," mewed Elizabeth mournfully, "and now it is all too late!"

Darcy looked at her with more feeling than he was sensible of expressing.

"How is such a cat as Wickham to be worked on?" cried Elizabeth. "Lydia has no papers, no pedigree, nothing to tempt him. He will surely abandon her to the streets and sewers and she will be lost to us forever!"

Mr. and Mrs. Gardiner soon returned, and, with one last grave look, Darcy hastily bid Elizabeth goodbye.

I will never see him again, thought Elizabeth. And she had never felt, until now when it was too late, that she could have loved him. Fate, reflected Elizabeth, as she and her aunt and uncle climbed into the carriage to return to Longbourn, is even more perverse than cats!

145

Darcy made no answer. He seemed scarcely to hear her, and was walking up and down the room in earnest meditation; his brow contracted, his air gloomy. Elizabeth soon observed, and instantly understood it. Her power was sinking; every thing must *sink under such a proof of family weakness, such an assurance of the deepest disgrace. She could neither wonder nor condemn, but the belief of his self-conquest brought nothing consolatory to her bosom, afforded no palliation of her distress. It was, on the contrary, exactly calculated to make her understand her own wishes; and never had she so honestly felt that she could have loved him, as now, when all love must be vain.*

Chapter Five

Upon reaching Longbourn, Elizabeth eagerly dashed inside to greet Jane and learn whether she had received any fresh intelligence from their father about Lydia's whereabouts in London. Jane replied that Mr. Bennet was in town but had no news of Lydia.

"But we are hoping to hear any day that they are safe at Gretna Green," she said. Jane then produced a letter Lydia had left for Mrs. Forster when she ran away with Wickham.

Mrs. Bennet, meanwhile, was in a dreadful state. Her fur was matted and her "mews" pitiful and profuse. "If only Mr. Bennet had taken us all to Brighton, this would not have happened!" she cried. "Why did the Forsters ever let her out of their sight? I'm sure there was some great neglect on their side, for she is not the kind of cat to run away. And now," she continued, "Mr. Bennet is gone away and I know he and Wickham will fight and Wickham will kill him! Then what is to happen to us all? The Collinses will turn us out and we will be left on our own to hunt mice in the hedgerows!"

Mr. Gardiner encouraged Mrs. Bennet to calm herself and assured her he would be in town the next day to assist Mr. Bennet in recovering Lydia.

"Oh, my dear brother," replied Mrs. Bennet, "that is exactly what I could most wish for, and above all, keep Mr. Bennet from fighting with Wickham!"

Mr. Bennet will fight and
Wickham will kill him!

"*MY DEAR HARRIET,*

"*You will laugh when you know where I am gone, and I cannot help laughing myself at your surprise to-morrow morning, as soon as I am missed. I am going to Gretna Green, and if you cannot*

guess with who, I shall think you a simpleton, for there is but one man in the world I love, and he is an angel. I should never be happy without him, so think it no harm to be off. You need not send them word at Longbourn of my going, if you do not like it, for it will make the surprise the greater, when I write to them, and sign my name Lydia Wickham. What a good joke it will be! I can hardly write for laughing.

Pray make my excuses to Pratt, for not keeping my engagement, and dancing with him to-night. Tell him I hope he will excuse me when he knows all, and tell him I will dance with him at the next ball we meet, with great pleasure. I shall send for my clothes when I get to Longbourn; but I wish you would tell Sally to mend a great slit in my worked muslin gown, before they are packed up. Good bye. Give my love to Colonel Forster, I hope you will drink to our good journey.

"Your affectionate friend,
"LYDIA BENNET."

*My Dear Harriet,
You will laugh when
you know where I am
gone...*

Chapter Six

MR. GARDINER SET off almost immediately for London in search of Lydia. He promised Mrs. Bennet to leave no rat uncornered (including Wickham himself) in his search for her, and to send Mr. Bennet home directly. The Bennet sisters were surprised that their mother did not appear gratified by this news, considering her anxiety about Mr. Bennet losing every one of his nine lives fighting with Wickham.

"What, is he coming home, and without poor Lydia?" cried Mrs. Bennet. "Who is to fight Wickham and make him marry her if he comes away?"

Mrs. Bennet could get no rest thinking of Wickham's wicked deeds.

In the meantime, all of Meryton was bent on blackening Wickham's character when, but a few months before, he had been the handsomest animal ever to grace the militia. Yet now there was nothing of an evil nature he was not guilty of. Poor Mrs. Bennet could get no rest thinking of Wickham's wicked deeds—brawls, nightly assignations with all the female cats in the county, even chicken killings. Everyone began to find out that they had never trusted his appearance of goodness. Wickham and Lydia, it was concluded, were well concealed in London, for neither Uncle Gardiner nor Mr. Bennet had succeeded in discovering them.

While Mr. Bennet was in London, the Bennets received a letter from their cousin, Mr. Collins, consoling them on the irremediable calamity that had befallen their family. This letter was followed by another from Mr. Gardiner who wrote to tell them that Mr. Bennet would be home the following day.

When Mr. Bennet did return to Longbourn, he had all the appearance of his usual philosophic composure.

"If I should ever go to Brighton, I would behave better than Lydia," announced Kitty, when they were having tea afterwards.

"You, go to Brighton?!" exclaimed Mr. Bennet. "I would not trust you so near it as Eastbourne for a hind quarter of pork! No, Kitty, I have at last learnt to be cautious and you will feel the effects of it. No cat in the militia is ever to enter into my house again, nor even to pass through the village. Balls will be absolutely prohibited, unless you roll them with one of your sisters. And you are never to stir out of doors till you can prove that you have spent ten minutes of every day in a rational manner."

Kitty, who took all these threats in a serious light, mewed long and plaintively.

"Well, well," said he, "do not make yourself unhappy. If you are a good kitten for the next ten years, I will take you to a review at the end of them."

Mr. Bennet had all the appearance of his usual philosophic composure.

"MY DEAR SIR,

"I feel myself called upon, by our relationship, and my situation in life, to condole with you on the grievous affliction you are now suffering under, of which we were yesterday informed by a letter from Hertfordshire. Be assured, my dear Sir, that Mrs. Collins and myself sincerely sympathise with you, and all your respectable family, in your present distress, which must be of the bitterest kind, because proceeding from a cause which no time can remove. No arguments shall be wanting on my part, that can alleviate so severe a misfortune; or that may comfort you, under a circumstance that must be of all others most afflicting to a parent's mind. The death of your daughter would have been a blessing in comparison of this. And it is the more to be lamented, because there is reason to suppose, as *my dear Charlotte informs me, that this licentiousness of behaviour in your daughter, has proceeded from a faulty degree of indulgence, though, at the same time, for the consolation of yourself and Mrs. Bennet, I am inclined to think that her own disposition must be naturally bad, or she could not be guilty of such an enormity, at so early an age. Howsoever that may be, you are grievously to be pitied, in which opinion I am not only joined by Mrs. Collins, but likewise by Lady Catherine and her daughter, to whom I have related the affair. They agree with me in apprehending that this false step in one daughter, will be injurious to the fortunes of all the others, for who, as Lady Catherine herself condescendingly says, will connect themselves with such a family. And this consideration leads me moreover to reflect with augmented satisfaction on a certain event of last November; for had it been otherwise, I must have been involved in all your sorrow and disgrace. Let me then advise you, my dear Sir, to console yourself as much as possible, to throw off your unworthy child from your affection for ever, and leave her to reap the fruits of her own heinous offense.*

"*I am, dear Sir, etc., etc.*"

Chapter Seven

SHORTLY AFTER MR. Bennet's return, Jane and Elizabeth were stalking a squirrel in the shrubbery, when Hill, the housekeeper, came to tell them that an express letter had arrived for their father from London. The two sisters dashed off to find their father and learn what news he had received.

The letter was from Uncle Gardiner to say that Lydia and Wickham had been apprehended, and that for a modest sum (100 mice per annum, per animal), their union would be finalized in as a respectable manner as any cat could hope for. And, apparently, the whole had been accomplished by their uncle!

"There are two things I want to know," said Mr. Bennet, frowning over the letter. "One is how much your uncle had to lay out to persuade Wickham to agree to these terms, and the other is, how am I ever going to repay him?"

When Mrs. Bennet heard the good news about her daughter, she became as violently exuberant (chasing an imaginary feather about her sitting room) as she had been alarmed and vexed before.

"But the feast, the wedding feast!" she cried.

She was proceeding to the particulars of chicken gizzards, mouse hearts, and fish heads, and would shortly have dictated some very plentiful orders had not Jane, though with some difficulty, persuaded her to wait till her father was at leisure to be consulted.

Elizabeth reflected that although with Wickham, Lydia could expect neither peaceful catnaps nor a prosperous home (for what humans would take them in now?), things had concluded much more advantageously than she had dared to hope only a few hours before.

After a slight preparation for good news, the letter was read aloud. Mrs. Bennet could hardly contain herself. As soon as Jane had read Mr. Gardiner's hope of Lydia's being soon married, her joy burst forth, and every following sentence added to its exuberance. She was now in an irritation as violent from delight, as she had ever been fidgetty from alarm and vexation. To know that her daughter would be married was enough. She was disturbed by no fear for her felicity, nor humbled by any remembrance of her misconduct.

"My dear, dear Lydia!" she cried. "This is delightful indeed!—She will be married!—I shall see her again!—She will be married at sixteen!—My good, kind brother!—I knew how it would be.—I knew he would manage everything! How I long to see her! and to see dear Wickham too! But the clothes, the wedding clothes! I will write to my sister Gardiner about them directly. Lizzy, my dear, run down to your father, and ask him how much he will give her. Stay, stay, I will go myself. Ring the bell, Kitty, for Hill. I will put on my things in a moment. My dear, dear Lydia!—How merry we shall be together when we meet!"

Chapter Eight

MR. BENNET HAD never dreamed that he and Mrs. Bennet would have no male offspring to cut off Mr. Collins's end-tail. Because he had always believed he would one day have a male heir, Mr. Bennet had put aside neither mice nor money for bribing worthless toms to make his equally worthless daughter respectable. Yet now he was indebted to Uncle Gardiner for doing just that. And he had no idea what stores of dry food Mr. Gardiner had been compelled to lay out to accomplish it!

The news of Lydia and Wickham's newly acquired respectability soon spread through the house and the neighborhood with equal rapidity. Mrs. Bennet, who had not stirred from her room in a fortnight, now leapt from her bed with alacrity and raced downstairs, where she immediately began speculating about homes in which Lydia and Wickham might reside.

"Haye Park might do," cried she, "if the humans could quit it— or the great house at Stoke, if the pawing-room were larger; but Ashworth is too far off! I could not bear to have her ten miles from me; and as for Purrvis Lodge, the attics are dreadful. Not even the mice will go near them!"

Elizabeth now began to wish that Darcy had never learned of Lydia's infamous elopement. But even if he were unaware of it, would he condescend to connect himself to such a family and to have Wickham as a brother-in-law? Elizabeth could not believe it and repined for his company and gentlemanly meows. She was convinced, now that it was too late, that he was the ideal match for her. Her lively disposition and playfulness must have intrigued and engaged him while his knowledge of mice and men would benefit her.

Lydia and Wickham were to be banished to the North of England. What a fate for poor Lydia! Mrs. Bennet could not resign herself to it. To make matters worse, Mr. Bennet was too angry with his daughter and Mr. Wickham to allow them to visit Longbourn before they left for the North. But gradually Jane and Elizabeth persuaded him to allow the couple to visit, though Elizabeth could not imagine how Wickham could present himself to her mother and father with equanimity.

So Jane Austen is going to be our new cook?

Random cat comments on *The Jane Austen Cookbook.*

[Elizabeth] *began now to comprehend that he was exactly the man, who, in disposition and talents, would most suit her. His understanding and temper, though unlike her own, would have answered all her wishes. It was an union that must have been to the advantage of both; by her ease and liveliness, his mind might have been softened, his manners improved; and from his judgement, information, and knowledge of the world, she must have received benefit of greater importance.*

But no such happy marriage could now teach the admiring multitude what connubial felicity really was. An union of a different tendency, and precluding the possibility of the other, was soon to be formed in their family.

How Wickham and Lydia were to be supported in tolerable independence, she could not imagine. But how little of permanent happiness could belong to a couple who were only brought together because their passions were stronger than their virtue, she could easily conjecture.

Chapter Nine

Nothing could equal Mrs. Bennet's triumphant trills on receiving her dear Lydia and her now-dear Wickham at Longbourn.

Elizabeth and Jane greeted Lydia in the hallway, after which Lydia raced about in a wilder manner than ever, demanding everyone's attention and notice. Was she not the luckiest cat in the kingdom? She, the youngest sister, to have found such a handsome partner as Wickham! Did not all her sisters envy her? Mrs. Bennet was scarcely less wild and noisy than Lydia, while her husband stood by looking grave and silent.

During the visit, Mrs. Bennet expressed her disappointment that Lydia and Wickham must remove so far from Longbourn.

"I don't at all like your going such a long way off," she added. "Must it be so?"

"Oh, lord! Yes; there is nothing in that," chirped Lydia. "I shall like it of all things. You and papa and my sisters must come down and see us. We shall be at Newcastle all the winter, and I dare say there will be plenty of balls, and I will take care to get some for my sisters."

"I should like that beyond anything!" cried her mother.

Lydia was exceedingly fond of her new mate. She groomed him and praised his sleek shiny coat and sharp claws. He did every thing best in the world, and she was sure he would kill more birds on the first of September than any other cat in the country.

During her visit, Lydia let it slip to Elizabeth and Jane that Mr. Darcy had been present at the church when she and Wickham joined paws in marriage.

Elizabeth was incredulous; Mr. Darcy present at the church? What was he doing there—he, of all cats? What could it mean? It was exactly a scene, among such creatures, where he had least temptation to go. Conjectures as to the meaning of it, rapid and wild, hurried through her brain; but she was satisfied with none.

Elizabeth could not rest until she knew it all, and she hastily sent an express letter to her aunt in London asking to know the particulars, if her aunt were at liberty to tell her.

And if she is *not* at liberty, thought Elizabeth, I shall certainly be reduced to stratagems and tricks to find it out.

"And *I* am Elizabeth Bennet."

161

"Lizzy, I never gave you an account of my wedding. . .
. . .

We were married, you know, at St. Clement's, because Wick-ham's lodgings were in that parish. And it was settled that we should all be there by eleven o'clock. My uncle and aunt and I were to go together; and the others were to meet us at the church. Well, Monday morning came, and I was in such a fuss! I was so afraid you know that something would happen to put it off, and then I should have gone quite distracted. And there was my aunt, all the time I was dressing, preaching and talking away just as if she was reading a sermon. However, I did not hear above one word in ten, for I was thinking, you may suppose, of my dear Wickham. I longed to know whether he would be married in his blue coat. . .

Well, and so just as the carriage came to the door, my uncle was called away upon business to that horrid man Mr. Stone. And then, you know, when once they get together, there is no end of it. Well, I was so frightened I did not know what to do, for my uncle was to give me away; and if we were beyond the hour, we could not be married all day. But, luckily, he came back again in ten minutes time, and then we all set out. However, I recollected afterwards, that if he had been prevented going, the wedding need not be put off, for Mr. Darcy might have done as well."

"Mr. Darcy!" repeated Elizabeth, in utter amazement.

"Oh, yes—he was to come there with Wickham, you know. But gracious me! I quite forgot! I ought not to have said a word about it. I promised them so faithfully! What will Wickham say? It was to be such a secret!"

Chapter Ten

ELIZABETH WAS VERY soon satisfied by receiving a long letter from her Aunt Gardiner, and promptly carried her treasure off to a little copse to peruse it in privacy. Her aunt began by expressing surprise that Elizabeth required an explanation for Mr. Darcy's presence at Lydia's wedding, implying that she, Aunt Gardiner, believed Elizabeth and Darcy to be on such intimate terms as to have no secrets between them.

Mrs. Gardiner went on to acquaint Lizzy with all that had happened concerning Mr. Darcy: Almost the next day after Elizabeth and the Gardiners quit Derbyshire, Darcy himself had left Pemberley and made his way to London. There, by sense and scents, he discovered where Lydia and Wickham were hiding. His motive for hunting them down was to compel Wickham to make his union with Lydia respectable. For their flight, Mr. Darcy felt he was solely to blame. Had he not been too proud to lay his private actions open to the world, Lydia would never have run away with Wickham. But Mr. Darcy had preserved a haughty silence; his upstanding cat character, he had believed, should speak for itself. Therefore, since he was responsible for the infamous and injurious elopement, he alone must be responsible for the remedy.

Mr. Darcy had first tried to persuade Lydia to return to her family, Mrs. Gardiner related, even offering her his most luxurious cat carrier to take her to Longbourn. But Lydia had declined; she was perfectly happy with her dear Wickham and needed none of Mr. Darcy's help. She was sure their match would be made respectable sometime or other, and it did not matter much when.

Mr. Darcy soon discovered that Wickham had very different feelings. He cherished the hope of a more advantageous match with another cat. In spite of this, he was receptive to Mr. Darcy's offer of a lifetime supply of wet food and a comfortable kennel to share with Lydia.

After Darcy acquainted Mr. and Mrs. Gardiner with all these particulars, Mr. Gardiner expressed his earnest desire of helping to pay for Wickham's keep. Mr. Darcy, however, showed himself to be as obstinate as a cat generally is and took all the trouble of arranging things between Lydia and Wickham himself.

Both Lydia and Wickham had access to the Gardiners' house while awaiting their final union. Aunt Gardiner had lectured her niece repeatedly in a most serious manner about the evil of running away with Wickham, but Lydia merely laid her ears back and pretended not to hear.

Her aunt concluded her letter by telling Elizabeth how very much she liked Mr. Darcy and how easy and pleasing his manners were. All he needed was playfulness and *that*, if chose his partner prudently, would not be lacking.

This letter threw Elizabeth into such a flutter of spirits that she had to roll around the grass and chase a rabbit into the underbrush before she could compose herself. Was Darcy's motive for putting to rights matters between Lydia and Wickham due only to mistaken pride? Or did he still harbor passionate feelings towards her? Elizabeth was trotting around the park, reflecting on this question, when Wickham caught up with her. He asked whether she had seen Mr. Darcy at Lambton and what she thought of his sister, Georgiana.

Elizabeth replied that she had seen Mr. Darcy and that she found his sister delightful, though rather shy. Wickham replied with a low growl. He went on to inquire if she had visited the village of Kympton. "I ask," he said, "because that was where old Mr. Darcy promised me a house in which to pass my days in pastoral tranquility. But, as you know, his son chose to disregard his late father's wishes. Oh, the snug parsonage with its sunny morning room and the many mice—how I would have loved it!"

"I heard," replied Elizabeth, "that you told Mr. Darcy that you did not wish to live a retired life and were compensated accordingly."

Wickham's eyes widened and he uttered a silent meow.

"Come, Mr. Wickham," said Elizabeth, "let us not quarrel about the past."

They then went inside, while Wickham tried to compose his features, and succeeded only in looking very silly.

Wickham, my dear, is that Mr. Darcy scratching at the door?

"I fancy, Lizzy, that obstinacy is the real defect of his character after all. He has been accused of many faults at different times, but this is the true one. Nothing was to be done that he did not do himself; though I am sure (and I do not speak it to be thanked, therefore say nothing about it), your uncle would most readily have settled the whole. They battled it together for a long time, which was more than either the gentleman or lady concerned in it deserved. But at last your uncle was forced to yield, and instead of being allowed to be of use to his niece, was forced to put up with only having the probable credit of it, which went sorely against the grain; and I really believe your letter this morning gave him great pleasure, because it required an explanation that would rob him of his borrowed feathers, and give the praise where it was due."

Chapter Eleven

POOR MRS. BENNET was reduced to a pitiable state when the time came for Lydia and Wickham to leave for the North. Her spirits remained low after their departure and she spent several days hiding under the bed. But then came news of a most promising nature; Mr. Bingley was expected back at Netherfield for a few weeks of bird hunting!

All Mrs. Bennet's former ambitions for Jane and Bingley were instantly reanimated. Jane pretended to be engrossed with a juicy fly, while her mother meowed noisily of her expectations, her schemes for her eldest daughter to spring on Mr. Bingley in the shrubbery, and her plans to invite him to dinner of chicken-flavored catnip and roasted mouse as soon as he came into the country.

On the third morning after his arrival in Hertfordshire, Mr. Bingley arrived at Longbourn, bringing with him Mr. Darcy! Elizabeth was agitated, surprised, and gratified by Darcy accompanying his friend. Her fur fluffed up and her eyes brightened at the thought that he still loved her. But she would not be secure; *Let me see how he behaves,* thought she.

She sat intently chewing on a bit of lace and did not dare to lift her eyes at first. When she did, she thought he looked grave and serious—more like the cat she had first known in Hertfordshire than the unreserved creature who welcomed them so warmly to Pemberley.

Mrs. Bennet bragged of her youngest daughter's match with Mr. Wickham.

"It is a delightful thing, to be sure," said Mrs. Bennet, "to have a daughter well married. They are gone down to Newcastle, to a kennel quite northward, it seems, and there they are to stay—I do not know how long. A very fine kennel it is, too." Mrs. Bennet fixed Mr. Darcy with an icy stare. "Thank Heaven! He has *some* friends, though perhaps not so many as he deserves," she said.

Elizabeth, who knew this to be leveled at Mr. Darcy, was in such misery of shame that she chewed her lace even more energetically. Mr. Darcy, to whom all her family were indebted!

Mrs. Bennet meanwhile drooled all over Mr. Bingley.

"When you have killed all your own birds, Mr. Bingley," she said, "I beg you will come here and kill as many as you please on Mr. Bennet's manor."

Before they went away, Mrs. Bennet secured both toms for an invitation to dinner. She had thought of asking them to dine that

day but she did not think anything less than two whole fish would satisfy the appetite of such a stately cat as Mr. Darcy.

* * *

"Oh! my dear Lydia," [Mrs. Bennct] cried, "when shall we meet again?"

"Oh, lord! I don't know. Not these two or three years, perhaps."

"Write to me very often, my dear."

"As often as I can. But you know married women have never much time for writing. My sisters may write to me. They will have nothing else to do."

I can't believe my own daughter unfriended me.

Mr. Wickham's adieus were much more affectionate than his wife's. He smiled, looked handsome, and said many pretty things.

"He is as fine a fellow," said Mr. Bennet, as soon as they were out of the house, "as ever I saw. He simpers, and smirks, and makes love to us all. I am prodigiously proud of him. I defy even Sir William Lucas himself, to produce a more valuable son-in-law."

The loss of her daughter made Mrs. Bennet very dull for several days.

"I often think," said she, "that there is nothing so bad as parting with one's friends. One seems so forlorn without them."

"This is the consequence you see, Madam, of marrying a daughter," said Elizabeth. "It must make you better satisfied that your other four are single."

169

Chapter Twelve

ELIZABETH DID NOT know how to interpret Mr. Darcy's silence and reserve. And yet, though he had not spoken, he had taunted her with a toy mouse by batting it her way and then recovering it himself. Elizabeth could not fathom his feelings.

"Teasing, teasing cat! I will think no more about him!"

On Tuesday the two toms came to dinner at Longbourn. To her satisfaction, Elizabeth saw that Mr. Bingley seated himself by her sister Jane at dinner, as he used to. Mrs. Bennet, meanwhile, continued her uncivil behavior to Mr. Darcy who, though rather grave, devoured a whole fish and two partridges.

After dinner, everyone repaired to the drawing room where Mrs. Bennet pressed her guests to catch goldfish, chase string, or play with cards. Mr. Darcy was not inclined to join in the latter, even when Kitty batted the Ace of Spades right under his nose. Soon afterwards the guests departed.

Anticipating the renewal of Mr. Bingley's addresses to Jane, Mrs. Bennet was in high spirits, while Jane endeavored to compose herself and persuade Lizzy that she was content to remain only his friend and companion.

**Mr. Darcy was not inclined to join the game, even when Kitty
batted the Ace of Spades right under his nose.**

Darcy had walked away to another part of the room. She followed
him with her eyes, envied everyone to whom he spoke, had scarcely
patience enough to help anybody to coffee; and then was enraged
against herself for being so silly!

"A man who has once been refused! How could I ever be foolish
enough to expect a renewal of his love? Is there one among the sex,
who would not protest against such a weakness as a second proposal
to the same woman? There is no indignity so abhorrent to their feelings!"

171

Chapter Thirteen

A FEW DAYS after this, Mr. Darcy left for town and Mr. Bingley trotted over the fields to call on the Bennets again. In fact, he came so early that none of the Bennet cats were fully awake. He stayed until after supper and came again the next morning to kill birds with Mr. Bennet. The two toms set off together to hide and pounce in the shrubbery, and had a fine sport of it. After this, Jane did not try to persuade Elizabeth that she and Mr. Bingley were merely friendly acquaintances.

The next evening after dinner, Elizabeth accidentally interrupted her sister and Mr. Bingley murmuring together near the hearth. Mr. Bingley quickly darted off towards Mr. Bennet's library. Purring ecstatically, Jane then confided her overflowing happiness and delight to Elizabeth: She and Mr. Bingley were to be united! They would not hide in London or run off to Gretna Green, but would form a union all their family could rejoice in and settle together at Netherfield.

Jane scampered away to tell her mother the good news. Elizabeth, left to herself, reflected that after all the Bingley sisters' falsehoods and contriving, and Mr. Darcy's interference, the affair had concluded happily for Mr. Bingley, Jane, and all the Bennet family.

"Oh! My dear, dear Jane, I am so happy!" cried Mrs. Bennet, after Mr. Bingley had taken leave. "I always said it must be so, at last. I was sure you could not be so beautiful for nothing! Why you

Elizabeth interrupted her sister and Mr. Bingley murmuring together near the hearth.

could have won first prize at the Westminster Cat Show! But now Bingley has won you, and that is even better."

Jane's younger sisters began to petition in their own interest. Mary requested use of the library at Netherfield—she loved nothing more than to nap on a book left open by its owner—while Kitty pleaded to play with Mr. Bingley's fine ball.

"I am certainly the most fortunate creature that ever existed!" trilled Jane to Elizabeth. "If I could but see you as happy! If there were but such another cat for you!"

The Bennets were speedily pronounced to be the luckiest cats in the country, though only a few weeks before, when Lydia had run away, they had been generally thought to be no better than common strays.

I saw another me around here somewhere

If I could but see you as happy! If there were but such another cat for you!

⁓⁓⊰❊⊱⁓⁓

He came, and in such very good time, that the ladies were none of them dressed. In ran Mrs. Bennet to her daughter's room, in her dressing gown, and with her hair half finished, crying out,

"My dear Jane, make haste and hurry down. He is come—Mr. Bingley is come—He is, indeed. Make haste, make haste. Here, Sarah, come to Miss Bennet this moment, and help her on with her gown. Never mind Miss Lizzy's hair."

"We will be down as soon as we can," said Jane; "but I dare say Kitty is forwarder than either of us, for she went up stairs half an hour ago."

"Oh! hang Kitty! what has she to do with it? Come be quick, be quick! Where is your sash, my dear?"

Chapter Fourteen

ONE MORNING, SHORTLY after Jane Bennet's engagement to Mr. Bingley, Lady Cat pounced upon Longbourn, chased by four hounds (who, it turned out, had made sport with her after she alighted from her carriage in Meryton). She entered the room with her hair on end and was most uncivil—positively catty—to Mrs. Bennet.

"You have a very small park here," she remarked after a short silence. "I doubt it affords enough rodents for your table."

"Our suppers are nothing in comparison of Rosings, my lady, I dare say," replied Mrs. Bennet, "but I assure you they are much more sumptuous than Sir William Lucas's."

Mrs. Bennet begged her ladyship to partake of a cat treat but Lady Cat declined with little civility; and then, arching her back, said to Elizabeth: "Miss Bennet, there seemed to be a prettyish kind of a little wilderness on one side of your lawn. I should be glad to take a romp in it, if you will favor me with your company."

Elizabeth could not imagine the purpose of such a romp— indeed, Lady Cat was not the romping sort. As it turned out, her ladyship had come with a warning—and an irresistible urge to sharpen her claws on the unsuspecting Elizabeth.

"You can be at no loss, Miss Bennet, to understand the reason of my journey hither," she began. "Your own heart, your own conscience, must tell you why I come."

As it turned out, Lady Cat had heard a rumor that her nephew Mr. Darcy had offered Elizabeth his paw in marriage. She arrived hoping to frighten Lizzy off with hisses and swipes. But Elizabeth showed herself equal to repelling these ill-natured attacks.

"Miss Bennet, I insist on being satisfied," Lady Cat demanded. "Has my nephew offered his paw in marriage?"

"Your ladyship has declared it to be impossible."

"It ought to be so; it must be so, while he retains the use of his reason. But your frisks and capers coupled with a fresh catnip harvest may have made him forget all he owes to himself and his family.

"Let me be rightly understood," Lady Cat continued. "Mr. Darcy is engaged to my daughter. From their kittenhood, they have been intended for each other. It was the favorite wish of his mother, as well as of hers. Even before they were able to open their eyes, we planned the union."

"If Mr. Darcy is neither by honor nor inclination confined to his cousin, why is not he to make another choice?" asked Elizabeth. "And if I am that choice, why may not I accept him?"

"Because pedigree, papers, prudence forbid it. My daughter and my nephew are formed for each other. They are descended, on the maternal side, from the same noble lion—I mean line; and, on the father's, from a respectable, honorable, and ancient breed."

Lady Cat then pressed Elizabeth to promise never to accept Mr. Darcy's proposal.

"I will make no promise of the kind," retorted Elizabeth.

"Miss Bennet I am shocked and astonished. I expected to find a more docile, domesticated cat."

"You have widely mistaken the character of my catness," growled Elizabeth, "if you think I can be worked on by such persuasions as these. I must beg, therefore, to be importuned no farther on the subject."

"Not so hasty, if you please, I am by no means done. To all the objections I have already urged, I have still another to add. I am no stranger to the particulars of your youngest sister's infamous elopement. I know it all. And is such a wild uncivilized animal to be my nephew's sister? Are the grounds of Pemberley to be thus polluted? Unfeeling, selfish cat!"

In this manner Lady Cat yowled on till they were at the door of the carriage, when, turning hastily round, she hissed: "I take no leave of you, Miss Bennet. I send no compliments to your mother. You deserve no such attention. I am most seriously displeased."

"Miss Bennet," replied her ladyship, in an angry tone, "you ought to know, that I am not to be trifled with. But however insincere you may choose to be, you shall not find me so. My character has ever been celebrated for its sincerity and frankness, and in a cause of such

Let me be rightly understood. This match, to which you have the presumption to aspire, can never take place. No, never. Mr. Darcy is engaged to my daughter.

177

moment as this, I shall certainly not depart from it. A report of a most alarming nature, reached me two days ago. I was told, that not only your sister was on the point of being most advantageously married, but that you, that Miss Elizabeth Bennet, would, in all likelihood, be soon afterwards united to my nephew, my own nephew, Mr. Darcy. Though I know it must be a scandalous falsehood; though I would not injure him so much as to suppose the truth of it possible, I instantly resolved on setting off for this place, that I might make my sentiments known to you."

"If you believed it impossible to be true," said Elizabeth, colouring with astonishment and disdain, "I wonder you took the trouble of coming so far. What could your ladyship propose by it?"

"At once to insist upon having such a report universally contradicted."

"Your coming to Longbourn, to see me and my family," said Elizabeth coolly, "will be rather a confirmation of it; if, indeed, such a report is in existence."

"If! do you then pretend to be ignorant of it? Has it not been industriously circulated by yourselves? Do you not know that such a report is spread abroad?"

"I never heard that it was."

"And can you likewise declare, that there is no foundation for it?"

"I do not pretend to possess equal frankness with your ladyship. You may ask questions, which I shall not choose to answer."

"This is not to be borne. Miss Bennet, I insist on being satisfied. Has he, has my nephew, made you an offer of marriage?"

"Your ladyship has declared it to be impossible."

"It ought to be so; it must be so, while he retains the use of his reason. But your arts and allurements may, in a moment of infatu-

ation, have made him forget what he owes to himself and to all his family. You may have drawn him in."

"If I have, I shall be the last person to confess it."

"Miss Bennet, do you know who I am? I have not been accustomed to such language as this. I am almost the nearest relation he has in the world, and am entitled to know all his dearest concerns."

"But you are not entitled to know mine; *nor will such behaviour as this, ever induce me to be explicit."*

Chapter Fifteen

Elizabeth was excessively discomposed by Lady Cat's ill-natured and unprovoked attack and could not refrain from some anxiety about her ladyship's influence on Mr. Darcy. How seriously, she wondered, did he depend on the advice of his alpha aunt, or rely upon her counsel? Did he, too, fear that Elizabeth would pollute the splendid woods of Pemberley?

If I don't see him at Longbourn again, she said to herself, *I will know how to understand it.*

The next morning, Mr. Bennet called Elizabeth into his library. He was amusing himself in batting a letter from Mr. Collins around the rug and kicking it with his paws. He invited Elizabeth to join in the fun.

The *contents* of the letter offered less sport for Elizabeth. Mr. Collins wrote to warn Lizzy against making a match with Mr. Darcy, as Lady Cat disapproved so strenuously.

"Mr. Darcy," wrote Mr. Collins, "possesses every thing a cat desires: splendid scratching trees, acres of soft dirt to dig in, noble pedigree. Yet in spite of all these temptations, let me warn my cousin Elizabeth, and yourself," he continued, "of the evils you may incur by a precipitate closure with this noble cat's advances, which of course, you will be inclined to take immediate advantage of."

He was amusing himself in batting a letter from Mr. Collins around the rug.

"Mr. Darcy!" marveled Mr. Bennet, "Who never looks at any female but to criticize a crooked tail or tattered ear, and who probably never looked at you in his life! It is admirable!"

Mr. Collins went on to express surprise that Mr. Bennet had welcomed Lydia and Wickham to Longbourn.

"You ought certainly to forgive them, but never to admit them in your sight, or allow their names to be mentioned in your hearing," he wrote.

"And he calls that forgiveness!" her father exclaimed.

Elizabeth recalled how her father had forgiven Kitty when she threw up a hair ball on the drawing room rug, and Mary when she scratched a favorite sofa to shreds, and could rejoice in her father's benevolence as well as his humor, though never had the latter been directed in a manner so scarcely agreeable to her.

"'Your daughter Elizabeth [Mr. Collins's letter continued], *it is presumed, will not long bear the name of Bennet, after her elder sister has resigned it, and the chosen partner of her fate, may be reasonably looked up to, as one of the most illustrious personages in this land.'*

"Can you possibly guess, Lizzy, who is meant by this? *'This young gentleman is blessed in a peculiar way, with every thing the heart of mortal can most desire,—splendid property, noble kindred, and extensive patronage. Yet in spite of all these temptations, let me warn my cousin Elizabeth, and yourself, of what evils you may incur, by a precipitate closure with this gentleman's proposals, which, of course, you will be inclined to take immediate advantage of.'*

"Have you any idea, Lizzy, who this gentleman is? But now it comes out."

"'My motive for cautioning you, is as follows. We have reason to imagine that his aunt, Lady Catherine de Bourgh, does not look on the match with a friendly eye.'

"Mr. Darcy, you see, is the man!"

ELIZABETH DID NOT have to wonder for long if she would see Mr. Darcy again; several days after Lady Cat's visit, he came to Longbourn with Mr. Bingley.

The two toms had been there only a short time when Bingley, who wanted to escape with Jane, proposed a walk. Elizabeth, Mr. Darcy, and Kitty joined them. Bingley and Jane soon lagged behind and Kitty ran down the lane to join Maria Lucas in a squirrel chase. Elizabeth then found herself alone with Mr. Darcy. She took the opportunity to express her gratitude for his help in restoring Lydia's reputation and respectability.

"If you will thank me," he replied, "let it be for yourself alone. Much as I respect your family, I believe I thought only of you." After a short pause, he added, "You are too generous to trifle with me. If your feelings are still what they were last April, tell me so at once. My affections and wishes are unchanged, but one word from you will silence my meows on this subject for ever."

Elizabeth then gave him to understand with chirps and trills that she welcomed his assurances of love and constancy with great pleasure. Mr. Darcy responded by rolling excitedly on his back— something Elizabeth had never known him to do before.

As they walked on, Darcy related that Lady Cat had visited him in London to complain bitterly about Elizabeth's obstinacy in refusing to refuse to marry him.

"It taught me to hope as I never had before," Darcy confessed.

Other than dictating, Lady Cat liked nothing more than being useful, Elizabeth reflected with amusement. And her usefulness in teaching her nephew to hope had never been better appreciated by Elizabeth than it was now.

He exposed himself as sensibly as a cat violently in love
can be supposed to do.

"If you will *thank me,"* [Darcy] *replied, "let it be for yourself alone. That the wish of giving happiness to you, might add force to the other inducements which led me on, I shall not attempt to deny.*

But your family *owe me nothing. Much as I respect them, I believe, I thought only of you."*

Elizabeth was too much embarrassed to say a word. After a short pause, her companion added, "You are too generous to trifle with me. If your feelings are still what they were last April, tell me so at once. My affections and wishes are unchanged, but one word from you will silence me on this subject for ever."

Elizabeth feeling all the more than common awkwardness and anxiety of his situation, now forced herself to speak; and immediately, though not very fluently, gave him to understand, that her sentiments had undergone so material a change, since the period to which he alluded, as to make her receive with gratitude and pleasure, his present assurances. The happiness which this reply produced, was such as he had probably never felt before; and he expressed himself on the occasion as sensibly and as warmly as a man violently in love can be supposed to do.

Chapter Seventeen

ELIZABETH AND DARCY wandered so long and happily down one lane and another that everyone was asking for them when they got back. Elizabeth worried that, in spite of his being such a handsome and prosperous tom, her family would not approve of her match with him, so disliked was Mr. Darcy for his proud, haughty manner and cuddling deficiencies.

At the first opportunity, Elizabeth acquainted Jane with her news.

"You are joking, Lizzy," said Jane. "This cannot be! Engaged to Mr. Darcy?!"

After a few playful frisks, Elizabeth settled down and assured her sister it was true. Mr. Darcy still loved her and they were indeed engaged.

* * *

"Good gracious!" cried Mrs. Bennet, as she stood at a window the next morning. "If that disagreeable Darcy-cat is not visiting again with our dear Bingley! What can he mean by being so tiresome as to be always coming here?"

Elizabeth and Darcy took to the lanes again and during their walk it was decided that the next cat to be made acquainted with their wishes was Mr. Bennet. To this end, Mr. Darcy slipped into Mr. Bennet's library after dinner. A short while later, her father called Elizabeth into the library. He was pacing back and forth across the room. "Lizzy," said he, "what are you doing? Are you out of your senses, to be accepting this cat? Have not you always hated him?"

How earnestly did Elizabeth then wish that her former opinions had been more reasonable, her meows more moderate! It would have spared her from professions which it was exceedingly awkward to give; but they were now necessary and she assured her father, with some confusion, of her attachment to Mr. Darcy.

"Or, in other words," Mr. Bennet replied, "you are determined to have him. He is rich, to be sure, and you may have finer toys and more sumptuous satin pillows than Jane. But will they make you happy?"

"Have you any other objection," asked Elizabeth, "than your belief of my indifference?"

"None at all. We all know him to be a proud, unpleasant sort of cat; but this would be nothing if you really liked him."

"I do, I do like him," she replied. "I love him."

Elizabeth went on to tell her father what a truly fine feline Mr. Darcy was, and to complete the favorable impression, she related what Mr. Darcy had voluntarily done for Lydia. Mr. Bennet heard her with astonishment.

"Had it been your uncle's doing," he assured her, "I must and would have paid him; but these violent young toms carry every thing their own way. I shall offer to pay him tomorrow; he will yowl and carry on about his love for you, and there will be an end of the matter."

Now Elizabeth had only to break the news to her mother. Its effect was most extraordinary; for on first hearing it, Mrs. Bennet sat quite still, unable to utter a syllable. She began at length to recover, to fidget about in her chair, jump down, jump up again, wonder aloud, and then wash herself.

"Mr. Darcy! Who would have thought it! And is it really true? Oh, my sweetest Lizzy! How rich and how great you will be! What dinners, what collars, what comfortable cat carriers you will have! Jane's is nothing to it—nothing at all. Such a charming cat! So handsome, so distinguished! Oh, my dear Lizzy, pray apologize for my having disliked him so much before. I hope he will overlook it."

Jane looked at her doubtingly. "Oh, Lizzy! it cannot be. I know how much you dislike him."

"You know nothing of the matter. That is all to be forgot. Perhaps I did not always love him so well as I do now. But in such cases as these, a good memory is unpardonable. This is the last time I shall ever remember it myself."

Miss Bennet still looked all amazement. Elizabeth again, and more seriously assured her of its truth.

"Good Heaven! can it be really so! Yet now I must believe you," cried Jane. "My dear, dear Lizzy, I would—I do congratulate you—but are you certain? forgive the question—are you quite certain that you can be happy with him?"

"There can be no doubt of that. It is settled between us already, that we are to be the happiest couple in the world. But are you pleased, Jane? Shall you like to have such a brother?"

"Very, very much. Nothing could give either Bingley or myself more delight. But we considered it, we talked of it as impossible. And do you really love him quite well enough? Oh, Lizzy! do any thing rather than marry without affection. Are you quite sure that you feel what you ought to do?"

"Oh, yes! You will only think I feel more than I ought to do, when I tell you all."

"What do you mean?"

"Why, I must confess, that I love him better than I do Bingley. I am afraid you will be angry."

"My dearest sister, now be *serious. I want to talk very seriously. Let me know every thing that I am to know, without delay. Will you tell me how long you have loved him?"*

"It has been coming on so gradually, that I hardly know when it began. But I believe I must date it from my first seeing his beautiful grounds at Pemberley."

I must date it from my first seeing his beautiful grounds at Pemberley.

ELIZABETH'S SPIRITS SOON rising to playfulness again, she spent the next morning cavorting in the copse with Mr. Darcy and teasing him about how he happened to become attached to her. She settled the matter nicely herself by supposing that her saucy nature, so different from that of other female cats who followed him everywhere, imitating his tastes and meowing pitifully when he was out of sight, was a refreshing change.

Both cats had news to communicate—Mr. Darcy to his aunt and Elizabeth to hers. This was soon done. Jane herself received a congratulatory letter from Caroline Bingley, but Elizabeth, looking over her sister's shoulder, detected several claw marks on it, which Jane kindly chose to overlook.

Georgiana's happiness in anticipating acquiring a sister was much more sincere and both Elizabeth and Darcy looked forward to all the comforts and coziness of their family party at Pemberley.

"My resolution of thanking you for your kindness to Lydia had certainly great effect [said Elizabeth]. *Too much, I am afraid; for what becomes of the moral, if our comfort springs from a breach of promise, for I ought not to have mentioned the subject? This will never do."*

"*You need not distress yourself. The moral will be perfectly fair. Lady Catherine's unjustifiable endeavours to separate us, were the means of removing all my doubts. I am not indebted for my present happiness to your eager desire of expressing your gratitude. I was not in a humour to wait for any opening of your's. My aunt's intelligence had given me hope, and I was determined at once to know every thing.*"

"*Lady Catherine has been of infinite use, which ought to make her happy, for she loves to be of use.*"

Anne, what the hell am I supposed to do with this stupid wedding veil?

Chapter Nineteen

SINCE BIRTH, MRS. Bennet had nursed and nudged, licked and lamented over her five kittens, and happy were her maternal feelings the day she got rid of her two most deserving—though it cannot be said that their brilliant matches taught her either delicacy or decorum.

Kitty improved as any kitty would who spends her time in the superior company of her two more sensible siblings. And although Lydia frequently tried to tempt her to visit with promises of toys and toms, Mr. Bennet would never consent to her going.

Mary alone of the five sisters stayed at home. Mrs. Bennet's love of company, however, compelled her daughter to socialize more and sleep less (although Mary had always professed to be philosophizing when her sisters caught her napping).

As for Lydia and Wickham, they lived a restless peripatetic life, moving from place to place in search of a cheaper kennel.

Miss Bingley, upon learning of Darcy's marriage, hissed and spat and was so ill-tempered that even her sister Louisa found her company insupportable. But, as she wished to retain the right to ramble the hills and halls of Pemberley, she took herself in paw and appeared at that great house disguised as an amicable cat.

Pemberley was now Georgiana's home and she and Elizabeth grew to love each other even as well as Darcy hoped they would.

Georgiana was occasionally alarmed at seeing how Elizabeth sported with Mr. Darcy, often tempting him to join her in a game of toss the mouse.

Lady Cat was extremely indignant at the marriage of Darcy. She eventually overcame her resistance to visiting Pemberley, however, and was seen sniffing about the woods, probably to ascertain the degree of pollution they had received from the presence of Elizabeth and the visits of her aunt and uncle from the city.

At Christmastime, the Darcys and the Gardiners could be seen curled up by the fireside, talking of the past and all that had happened—of purr and petulance, pride and prejudice, and the perfect happiness and harmony of the family party now gathered together at Pemberley.

Lady Catherine was extremely indignant on the marriage of her nephew; and as she gave way to all the genuine frankness of her character, in her reply to the letter which announced its arrangement, she sent him language so very abusive, especially of Elizabeth, that for some time all intercourse was at an end. But at length, by Elizabeth's persuasion, he was prevailed on to overlook the offence, and seek a reconciliation; and, after a little farther resistance on the part of his aunt, her resentment gave way, either to her affection for him, or her curiosity to see how his wife conducted herself; and she condescended to wait on them at Pemberley, in spite of that pollution which its woods had received, not merely from the presence of such a mistress, but the visits of her uncle and aunt from the city.

With the Gardiners, they were always on the most intimate terms. Darcy, as well as Elizabeth, really loved them; and they were both ever sensible of the warmest gratitude towards the persons who, by bringing her into Derbyshire, had been the means of uniting them.

About the Authors

The authors in another era.

PAMELA JANE is the author of over twenty children's books published by Houghton Mifflin, Atheneum, Simon & Schuster, Harper, and others. Her new children's book, *Little Elfie One*, illustrated by *New York Times* best-selling illustrator, Jane Manning, will be out from Harper in 2015. She is a writer and editor for *womensmemoirs.com*, and her own memoir, *An Incredible Talent for Existing: A Writer's Story*, will be published in 2016. Like Jane Austen, Pamela is a desperate walker and, unlike Jane, a terrible piano player. Visit her at *Pamelajane.com* and *Prideandprejudiceandkitties.com*.

DEBORAH GUYOL, a lawyer, is co-author of *The Complete Guide to Contract Lawyering*. She edits a legal publication, teaches creative writing, and conducts writing workshops (*www.letsgowrite.com*). Her photography studies were with Larry Sultan, Judy Dater, and Ellen Brooks, and her photographs have appeared in print and web publications. She has loved the novels of Jane Austen since she was a teenager and believes she has finally committed *Pride and Prejudice* to memory. Her current cats, Dexter and Dudley, do not share her literary and artistic interests.

Acknowledgments

WITH SPECIAL THANKS to:

Mittens, for making us laugh, and Annelise Bell for laughing with us.

John Bell, for staying behind in Florence to take care of Mittens when he got sick. (We know that was hard, John!)

Dudley and Dexter, despite the fact that they declined abundant opportunities to model for this book.

Kathryn Hathaway for her outstanding graphic design skills, and for hanging in there through dozens of long nights and many more drafts.

Sally Keehn for her outstanding photographs of authentic Regency settings.

Our intrepid agent, James McGinniss, for accomplishing the impossible.

Our editor, Marianna Dworak, for her wisdom, patience, and support.

Edward and Pheruze Pell, for their friendship and support through many incarnations of the manuscript.

Karen Karbo, for believing in our project from the start.

George Arrick, the best teacher and friend a girl ever had.

Writing friends—Pat Brisson, Deborah Heiligman, Sally Keehn, Joyce McDonald, Pamela Swallow, Kay Winters, and Elvira Woodruff, for friendship, support, and laughter.

Oregon Women Lawyers and its amazing listserve, the source of many of our kitty models.

JASNA's Oregon and Southwest Washington chapter, helping to keep Jane's flame burning.

And each other, because neither one of us could have created this book alone. Thanks for the friendship, imagination, persistence, and steadfast devotion to "follies and nonsense, whims and inconsistencies."

Extra big thank-yous to all the beautiful and beloved cats we photographed, as well as their generous and patient owners. You're all superstars!

Cats	Their obedient servants
Jake	Connie and Doug McDowell
Abby, Toby	Kathy Foldes
Thadeus	Pierre Robert
Cleo, Zima	George and Carolyn Vogt
Charger	Faye and Brian Meyer
Louie, Nala	Stu, Lori, Kate, and Anna Kesilman
Spooky	Tamara and Tony Solometo
Tabatha	Tess and Peter LaMontagne
Tessie	Anne and Steve Cooney
Samson, Mica	Denise Gour and Jim Neidhardt
Linus, Lucy	Nancy Palmer
Herman, Federico	Colleen Strohm
Oppenheimer, Leroy Brown	Laura Wood
Seamus O'Leary	Chris Fletcher and Mitch Finnegan
Aubrey, Io, Lindoro	Jeff and Jessie King
Pace Kittehmanz	Carla and Mike Drain
Francis	Anna Beaty
Captain, Lieutenant	Charlotte Rains Dixon

Rocky	LeeAnn Kriegh
Substance P, Little Lord Fauntleroy	Sarah Hickerson
Cleo, Dante	Amy, Patrick and Mackenzie Angel
Sam	Julie Entrekin
Percy, Kita	Gillian Bunker
Remy, Fat Cat	Rebecca Cambreleng
Angel	Nichole Tyska
Oscar	Ellen Theodorson
Diego, Emma, Ocho	Kim Upham
Georgie, Hook	Alana Iturbide
Mr. H, Rigby, Clovis, Rounder	Leah Koss and Drew Feldon
Mac	Tasha Lyn Cosimo and Matt Mitchell
Ashley	Beth and Steve Ferrarini
Lira, Austen	Tenley and Michael Cronan
Lexi, Earl	Devon Newman
Zoey, Cooper	Kim Fujinaga
Winter	Channa Newell
Pixie	Maggie Biondi
Tab	George and Pam Coffer
Mae West	Angela Sanders

Doodle Bug	Kathyn Vaughan
Kermit, Professor Pickles	Kim Pickett
Alfie	Melissa Walton and Trevor Hendricks
Peaches, Dasher, Dusty, Heidi, Desi, Angel, Cottontail, Miley	Vonnie Alto